Arianna Snow's
Novels
The Lochmoor Glen Series

Patience, My Dear is an enthralling, well crafted, superbly written 'page-turner' of a read, fruitfully exposed to the impairing remembrance and encounter of a first young love when nearing mid-life many years later. *Patience, My Dear* is very strongly recommended for readers searching for a superbly authored telling of an intricate and entertaining tale involving a love consumed memory and an ever-deepening mystery."

"A comedy of errors held together with taut suspense and biting dialogue, *My Magic Square* is a delicious pleasure from beginning to end. Naomi, the heroine of *Patience, My Dear*, also returns in this "must-read" sequel for all who delighted in the previous volume."

"Unwelcome visitors make their residence nearby, and there's a reason why they're unwelcome. *Threaded Needles* follows two amateur detectives whose bond of blood is unbreakable as they try to find out just what suspicious character Ian MacGill and his associate are planning. The resulting adventure is entertaining and enthralling. *Threaded Needles* is highly recommended for community library mystery collections."

"Dreams are to be treasured as they are pursued, and mourned when they are lost. *'Blessed Petals'* is a novel of dreams, and how some succeed, while others are shattered. A compelling human drama unfolds, making *'Blessed Petals'* a very solidly recommended read."

"*Without a Sword*" is another entry into the Lochmoor Glen series, and does the series justice."

"Another exciting thriller from Arianna Snow, "*Kade*" is not a read to be missed for fans of the series."

—Midwest Book Review

Please, Tell Me

A NOVEL

Arianna Snow

Golden Horse Ltd.
Cedar Rapids, Iowa

This book is primarily a book of fiction. Names, characters, places and incidents are either products of the author's imagination or actual historic places and events which have been used fictitiously for historical reference, as noted.

An Original Publication of Golden Horse Ltd.
P.O. Box 1002
Cedar Rapids, IA 52406-1002 U.S.A.
www.ariannaghnovels.com
ISBN 10: 0-977230880
ISBN 13: 978097230884

Library of Congress Control Number: 2010935427
First Printing
Volume 9 of *The Lochmoor Glen Series*

Printed and bound in the United States of America
by Publishers' Graphics, LLC

Cover: by Arianna Snow
        Photography by R.E, McClenahan
        Printed by White Oak Printing, Lancaster, PA

HIRAM GEOFFREY MCDONNALLY
FAMILY TREE

PATERNAL GRANDPARENTS
CAPTAIN GEOFFREY EDWARD MCDONNALLY
CATHERINE NORTON MCDONNALLY

FATHER
CAPTAIN GEOFFREY LACHLAN MCDONNALLY

UNCLE
EDWARD CALEB MCDONNALLY

MATERNAL GRANDPARENTS
ALEXANDER THOMAS SELRACH
SARAH GLASGOW SELRACH

MOTHER
AMANDA SELRACH MCDONNALLY

SISTER
HANNAH RUTH MCDONNALLY

NIECE
SOPHIA RUTH SIERZIK

HUSBAND: RAHZVON M. SIERZIK

BROTHER: GAELON SIERZIK

CARETAKERS
ALBERT ZIGMANN
ELOISE ZIGMANN

SON - GUILLAUME ZIGMANN

FRIEND: TRINA DUNMORE

FRIENDS
DANIEL O'LEARDON

LIVIA NICHOLS

NAOMI BEATRICE (MACKENZIE) MCDONNALLY FAMILY TREE

PATERNAL GRANDPARENTS
JEREMIAH NORMAN MACKENZIE
OCTAVIA HILL MACKENZIE

FATHER
NATHAN ELIAS MACKENZIE
DAGMAR ARNOLDSON MACKENZIE (STEPMOTHER)

MATERNAL GRANDPARENTS
JAMES HENRY SMITHFIELD
IRENE CLEBOURNE SMITHFIELD

MOTHER
BEATRICE SMITHFIELD MACKENZIE (Birdie)

BROTHER
JEREMIAH JAMES MACKENZIE

DAUGHTER
ALLISON SARAH O'CONNOR

HUSBAND
EDWARD CALEB MCDONNALLY

HALF-BROTHER
HENRY STRICKLAND (SON OF CECIL AND BEATRICE)
    WIFE: PEARL   SONS: MARVIN, CONRAD

FRIENDS
HARRIET DUGAN
JOSEPH DUGAN
HENRY MCTAVISH (Tavy)

MARYANNE AND BRUCE WHEATON
    DAUGHTERS:
    WILMOTH, MARVEL, CORINNE, JEANIE, DARA, MARTHA

The Chapters

Chapter 1

"The Gown"

"Our greatest glory is not in never falling,
but in rising every time we fall."

—Confucius

Eloise Zigmann, Hiram McDonnally's housekeeper, fled from the cottage through the garden gate leading to the main house. She glanced to the once-clear sky, distressed to see a dark front moving in from the west. Juggling three baskets of food, she managed to open the backdoor where she met Livia, Hiram's future intended.

"Dear me, Miss Nichols, I am afraid the weather is making a turn for the worst."

Livia relieved Eloise of two of the baskets and carried them into the kitchen. "Eloise, I had so hoped that it would be a beautiful day for the christening."

"'Tis a pity," Eloise agreed wiping her feet on the rug.

Livia lifted the linen cloth covering one of the baskets and peeked inside. "Hiram and I truly appreciate all of the trouble that you went to in making these additional afters."

"Never you mind—it was my pleasure. I had nothing better to do last night. It was actually quite pleasant; Albert entertained me with his fiddling, while I baked."

Livia looked beneath the other cloths. "I don't see the baby's gown?"

"Not to worry, Guillaume's bringing it. I did not want to risk wrinkling it, by trying to carry it with all of this. He should be here in a minute."

Livia opened the pendant watch, pinned on her dress bodice. "That's good because we should be leaving for the church in the next few minutes."

"Where is the little guest of honor?"

"Hiram is playing with him in the parlor. He is so proud to have Kade for a son. This adoption will be a blessing for all of us."

"Yes, Mum. You and Kade have changed the

master's view of the world considerably."

"Well, I shall get the baby and start undressing him."

Eloise nodded, looked out the window toward the back gate, and frowned when there was no sign of her son, Guillaume.

Guillaume stood over the kitchen basin in the cottage, scrubbing the ink-stained gown with the speed of a frantic dog digging for a bone. The indigo ink from his new pen was now turning the basin, his hands, and the bar of lye soap, an ominous blue. He clenched his teeth while he dipped the gown into the basin, again. Before wringing it out, he rinsed it in the bucket of pale blue water next to him. More blue drops fell to the pail as he gently squeezed the fabric. To his further dismay, when he shook out the tattered garment, pieces of lace fell to the water. He grimaced seeing a small, bow float over to the side of the bucket, dropped the spoiled dress back into the water, and dried his hands. He tossed the flour sack dishtowel to the table. With one stained hand on his hip, he anxiously massaged his forehead with the other.

"Blasted pen. My life is over," he muttered. "It is just a matter of who will end it first—Hiram or Mother." He jumped with a start when his mother entered the room, demanding, "Son, please, tell me— what are you doing and where is the gown?"

Guillaume hesitated, swallowed, and then pointed to the bucket. Eloise fearfully viewed the rippling layers.

"Agh! What have you done?" she screamed in horror.

"Mother, it was an accident. My pen and—"

"It is destroyed!" She covered her mouth.

"I am sorr—"

"Guillaume Zigmann, you have ruined the christening. Miss Nichols will be devastated; the master will have your hide! Was it not enough that the weather is not cooperating?"

Standing over the pail, Eloise frantically nibbled her nails. "What am I to do? This gown was sent from Switzerland—the master ordered it special for the occasion." She began to tremble. Breathing hard, she grasped the side of the table. Guillaume placed an arm around her shoulder.

"Mother, are you ill?"

Eloise jerked around. "Of course I am! I am sick to death of your irresponsible behavior!"

Guillaume stepped back, shocked by her brashness.

"Get out, Guillaume—out of my sight!"

Guillaume's heart sank. His mother had been disappointed with his behavior in the past when he was a child, but never to this degree.

Livia and Hiram stood at the window of the main house, observing Guillaume darting across the pasture, toward the barn.

"Something is wrong, Hiram," Livia handed the squirming, half-dressed infant to him. "Here, take the baby. I am going to the cottage." She quickly wrapped the blanket tightly around the baby's torso.

"What is going on?" Sophia, Hiram's newly married niece asked, standing in the doorway.

"I am not sure. I am going to find out," Livia said, opening the backdoor. Sophia followed Livia through the misting rain.

Upon entering the cottage, they heard Eloise sobbing. Within seconds, the source of her anxiety was apparent. Sophia stood mouth opened in shock, as Livia lifted the remnants of the gown from the bucket with a wooden spoon. Eloise continued to cry, feeling terribly responsible for her son's blunder.

"Was he dying it blue?" Sophia asked in disbelief.

Eloise cried even louder. Livia dropped the gown back to the water. "Now, now, Eloise, it is not important; we will just purchase another gown and postpone the christening. Look, it is a terrible day to take out the baby; it is pouring now."

Sophia stood speechless as her gaze moved from the ink-stained tablecloth, to the basin, to the bucket. She shook her head. "Men," she muttered. "But what about all of the people who are waiting at the church?"

Livia gave Sophia a brief disapproving glare, "They will be notified, Sophia."

Eloise was still sobbing uncontrollably when her husband Albert arrived. "The carriages are waiting. Elly, what is wrong?" He ran to her side. "Is it Guillaume? Is he all right?"

"He shan't be when I get a hold of him," she threatened between sobs.

Sophia raised her brows and cocked a signaling gaze to the disaster behind her. "The christening gown," she announced.

Albert scanned the area and then stepped to the bucket and peered inside. He gulped. His fists tightened, his face was beet red when he turned to Eloise. "Guillaume?"

Eloise wiped her eyes and nodded.

Albert, at a loss for words, shuddered, and looked painfully to Livia.

"It is not important, Albert. As I told Eloise, the day is not favorable for such a special occasion... with the rain and all. We will have the ceremony in the near future. Now, come along, Sophia, we need to send word to the church. These things happen for good reason. Someday, we will understand."

Albert put his arm around Eloise. "I am sorry, Miss Nichols. These things *always* happen with my son and there is never a *good* reason."

Livia forced a smile. She and Sophia hustled back to the house with their arms above their heads to ward off the driving rain.

"This situation is serious," Sophia remarked, swiping the drops from her sleeves, as she followed Livia into the house.

"*Sophia*, I said it is not important!"

"I beg your pardon? Please, do not reprimand me. It was not *I* who turned the baby's gown into a disgusting rag! Besides, I am a married woman now; I should be treated with respect—*you* are not even married!"

"Here, here, Sophia—watch your tongue!" Hiram cut in.

"Men! This is all because of your silly gender!" Sophia stormed out.

"Oh, Hiram." Livia started to cry.

"Where is Kade's gown?"

"Hiram, forget the blasted gown! He does not need it." Livia fled down the hall and up the stairs.

Hiram, totally confused, looked down at the smiling infant.

"Well, son, I guess you will be showing off your massive chest to the congregation. A little unconventional, but they might as well see you as a true McDonnally."

Sophia flew through the bedroom door where her husband, Rahzvon, stood at the window. "Phia, it is raining cats and dogs."

"Can you not see that I am drenched? That

Livia makes me *so* angry!"

Rahzvon turned to face her. "Livia? She is as gentle as a lamb."

"How dare you take her side—you traitor!"

"Traitor? Would you care to clarify that accusation?"

"No! I am tired of being treated like an infant— I am a married woman!"

"You do not have to remind *me*."

"This is serious, Mr. Sierzik!"

"Whatever it is, *Mrs. Sierzik*, forget it for now— we need to get downstairs. Do you need to change your dress?"

"We are not going."

"Not going? We will be thrown out of the clan— banished from Scotland. This is a once in a lifetime event. Dare you insult Livia and your Uncle?"

"It has crossed my mind. If you heard the manner in which *he* spoke to me—how *she* spoke to me...I don't think I want to be a McDonnally anymore," she pouted.

"You're not. You are a Sierzik." He took her hand. "Now, let's go before we no longer have a roof over our heads."

"That *Livia*—" A slight rapping at the jarred door gave her pause. Rahzvon opened it wider.

"May I please speak with Sophia," Livia asked humbly.

"Certainly. I will leave you two to resolve this, but you had better hurry. We are supposed to be on our way to the church."

"It doesn't matter. I am not going," Livia explained as she closed the door behind her.

Not going? Rahzvon took a breath, imagining Hiram's response and reconsidered going downstairs. Instead, he headed to the east wing.

"Sophia, I have come to apologize. I am so very sorry that I spoke to you in that manner. I offer no excuse."

As Sophia's mood made a full swing, she stepped over to Livia and offered her hand. "I understand. You must be terribly disappointed."

Livia sighed, looking forlorn. "I wanted this day to be perfect for your uncle."

"I know, but we shall prepare an even grander celebration. Besides, we needed more flowers in the church and perhaps, instead of such a frilly feminine gown, Eloise can make Kade a tiny kilt."

Livia cracked a smile. "Perhaps she can."

They embraced and walked down to the kitchen where Eloise's whimpering met them. Hiram was pacing with the baby who was whining, as well.

"Livy, please help. Make her stop!" Hiram pleaded.

Livia rushed to the distraught housekeeper. "Eloise, everything is fine."

"No it is not. Guillaume has left," she sobbed.

"I will find him," Sophia volunteered. "Which direction has he gone?"

"Toward the village," Eloise sniffled.

"I need to explain to those at the church, anyway."

"Miles can do that!" Hiram stepped from the kitchen and called from the hall.

"No, it would be better if a family member handled it!" Sophia returned, closing the main door behind her.

Keeping a watchful eye for Guillaume, Sophia continued on to the church. The horses hitched on the perimeter, stirred when she trotted up. She dismounted, straightened her skirt, and brushed back the black renegade curls dangling before her eyes. She slowly opened the heavy church door. Hearing the familiar voice echo from the altar, she slipped inside and took a seat in the back pew.

Guillaume spoke from behind the podium, "Are there any questions?"

Joseph Dugan's hand went up.

"Yes, Mr. Dugan?"

"What kind o' pen was it, lad?"

Harriet gave her husband a sharp elbow jab to his ribs.

Guillaume cocked his head in surprise to the trivial inquiry. "Uh...a Shaeffer, Mr. Dugan."

Little Marvin's hand shot up. Pearl, his mother, looked curiously at her son.

"Yes, Marvin?" Guillaume asked.

"What's yer punishment? Is yer Papa goin' to take a stick to ye?"

This stirred a few giggles from the younger children. Guillaume's deadpan expression silenced the room.

"No, Marvin, I am a bit old for that, but my parents *are* angry. I believe that they are more disappointed than upset. My mother was crying. You see, when a child does something that adversely affects those people who your parents love and respect—it hurts them, as well. It is their embarrassment, too. I failed to think before I acted. Now, my punishment is the memory of this day. I have caused a great inconvenience and disappointment for the McDonnallys and their friends in having to postpone the ceremony. I will have to live with the sadness and shame that I have brought to my family. Remember, Marvin, as should all of you children—you shall pay for the consequences of your actions. 'As you sow, so shall you reap'."

Hmm? Sophia bit her bottom lip. She noted that many adults, too, exchanged thoughtful looks in regard to Guillaume's warning.

Guillaume scanned the crowd of sympathetic faces. "I take full responsibility and humbly ask for your forgiveness."

Sophia observed their reaction; everyone was obviously moved by his sincere confession. Even Dagmar, stoic that she was, dried her eyes with her hankie. This was Sophia's cue. She sprinted down the aisle, hugged him, and whispered into his ear, "I am so honored that you are my friend."

At that moment, the pews emptied. Everyone joined her to offer sympathy to the courageous orator.

On the stroll from the church, Sophia walked proudly on Guillaume's arm.

"What story did you tell them, Mr. Zigmann?" Sophia teased.

"The truth, of course."

"And what might that be?" Sophia grinned.

"That I was up all night helping mother bake the afters. When she was too tired to sew a loose button on the gown, I offered. Naturally, my weary eyes were suffering from lack of sleep and I pricked my finger with the needle, thus soiling the gown with a dab of blood."

Sophia gave Guillaume a playful shove. "You are incorrigible. Honestly, I realize that confessing had to be difficult."

"The lesser of two evils, my friend. My confession was entirely more bearable than would be my parents' wrath, had I not done so."

They exchanged knowing smiles and mounted their horses.

***

Over the next two weeks, plans for another christening, and the order for a replacement gown, brightened the atmosphere at the McDonnally estate. Guillaume and his parents had made amends, but the gown mishap was not soon forgotten. Guillaume went to extraordinary lengths to be cautious in handling indigo ink. His mother took care in assigning duties for him, which required a great deal of responsibility.

Before breakfast, Sophia finished dressing behind the screen.

"Rahzvon, you need not worry so much about the care for our future children, our nanny will handle all of the distasteful tasks."

"What nanny?"

"Our nanny. With my trust fund and your inheritance, we shall definitely be in the position to hire a nanny."

"There will be no nanny."

"Why not?" Sophia scowled.

"It goes against Kosdreven code."

"What code?" she asked, while slipping on her skirt.

"The care of all children is to be provided solely by the natural parents, except in case of illness or an emergency trip. In case of death, the children are made wards of the nearest relative."

She stepped into view. "What about little lads like Kade, with no blood relatives?"

"He would become a charge of the queen."

"We are not living in Kosdrev, Rahzvon. In Scotland, people of fair income employ a nanny to assist them."

"I took an oath; I cannot break it," he

explained, pulling on his socks. "All Kosdrevians take the oath when they reach adulthood."

Sophia sat down at the dressing table. "No nanny? Any other oaths that I should be made aware of—*now that we are married*?"

"Several—that is why most Kosdrevians marry other Kosdrevians." He opened the door.

"Perhaps you should have married one of your *own* kind." She scrunched up her nose.

Rahzvon grinned mischievously. "That is of no consequence, because you, m' lady, shall behave no differently than your above-average, Kosdrevian, subservient wife." He quickly closed the door behind him.

Sophia held up her hairbrush, ready to hurl it towards the door. She thought better of it, but sent it flying just the same.

"Oaths," she muttered, finding the handle separated from the bristled part of her brush. "Thank you, Mr. Sierzik—that was my favorite hairbrush!"

At the breakfast table, Gaelon, Rahzvon's visiting, older brother and Hiram's twin, Hannah—Sophia's mother, were discussing life in the restaurant business when Sophia arrived. Kade was playing quietly in the basket and Rahzvon was boldly sitting in Hiram's chair at the head of the table. All greeted Sophia as Rahzvon helped her with her chair.

"Where are Uncle Hiram and Livia?" Sophia inquired while spooning out a fair portion of the ham soufflé.

"They have gone for a ride," Hannah replied, passing the toast.

"I wonder if he is planning to propose," Sophia snickered.

Everyone resigned from comment; they, too, were baffled by Hiram's avoidance of the inevitable.

Sophia turned to Rahzvon's brother. "Gaelon, could you please enlighten me on the archive of Kosdreven oaths?"

Gaelon wiped his mouth with his napkin. "I am confused as to why you ask. Surely, my brother informed you, before you agreed to marry him," he said with concern.

"He most certainly did *not!*" She flashed a disapproving look toward her husband.

"Hmm? In that case, where shall I begin? He did tell you about the forbidden nanny rule?"

"Yes, that he did." She rolled her eyes.

"Good. Most women of high society have a difference of opinion. All right, let me think...there are so many. You shall have to bear with me; I have been removed from the culture for some time."

Sophia anxiously tightened her lips.

"There is the one, where after the first month of marriage...the wife must read to her husband from the Kosdreven Book of History...twice a day. Ah, that may be of some difficulty for you, as it is in gisaleon."

Rahzvon tended to his meal without looking up.

"Why can he not read it himself?" She scowled at Rahzvon.

"That is the law, Sophia. The man must be in a prone position, free from disturbances, so that he might absorb the information."

"I beg your pardon? That is ridiculous!" Sophia glanced at Rahzvon, who shrugged innocently.

Gaelon continued, "The reading only requires approximately...two hours a day. It will be a good method for you to learn the language," he added with a positive tone. "Oh, yes, I forgot. After the ninth day of marriage, the wife must clean her husband's ears every morning from that day on. Ah, you may be a bit tardy on that one." He raised a brow.

"Clean his ears? That is outrageous!" She looked over at her mother, who shook her head.

Gaelon explained, "Not really, Sophia. In Kosdrev there are tiny insects that like to bed down in the ears at night."

"Well, we have no such insects in Scotland," Sophia defended.

"I am afraid that location is not an issue. It is an important ritual that must be performed," Gaelon said matter-of-factly.

"What about the oaths for the men?" Sophia sat up.

"Ah, yes, there are many," Gaelon replied.

Sophia smiled smugly. "Let us hear them."

"The husband must remind the woman of her daily duties... each day at dawn."

"What! At dawn?"

"Yes, he must awaken her and read from the official list of eighteen tasks," Gaelon pointed out.

"Eighteen! What if she has been up all night with the children?" Sophia protested.

"It does not matter—he has to notify her. Besides, this is her wakeup call. She will need to get to work while he gets the rest of his much needed sleep."

"You mean to say, that your brother is going to wake me up before sun-up and instruct me in my chores, so that he may enjoy the comforts of another few hours sleep?" She stood up, shoving her chair backward.

Rahzvon winked at Gaelon, "No, not *before* sun-up, Phia. *At* sun-up," Rahzvon corrected.

Sophia's intense black eyes pierced his. It was silent and then Rahzvon and Gaelon broke into uncontrolled laughter.

"Why are you laughing?" Sophia demanded. "Mother? Tell them this is not amusing—this is serious!"

"Sophia, my dear daughter, I believe that you have been the object of a clever, but dangerous, practical scheme."

"Scheme?" she frowned.

Gaelon caught his breath. "Sorry, Sophia, my brother put me up to fabricating those rules," he snickered.

Sophia's head turned slowly toward her husband. Rahzvon predicted her next move and suddenly left his chair. With Sophia in hot pursuit, he fled down the hall. After a slight skirmish in the parlor, Rahzvon, under duress, confirmed that the only actual oath that Gaelon mentioned was the nanny rule.

"Fortunate for you, sir, or you should have had to find another wife," Sophia announced.

"Ah, but Sophia we are locked together for eternity and there *are* a few important tenets of which you must abide." Rahzvon pulled her down next to him on the divan. "Phia, knowing you, you are not going to be too happy with these. I probably should have told you in advance."

"What *now*, Rahzvon?" Sophia sat up.

"It is mandatory for Kosdrevian men to take a second wife after the third year," he looked to the floor, then quickly up to her infuriated expression.

"Only teasing!" he reassured.

She grabbed the bolster and hit him, then dropped back under his arm, "I nearly had heart failure. Could you please stick to the facts?"

"Very well. Phia, this is in all seriousness. This may sound medieval, and quite inappropriate for this century."

"Sounds grand, thus far," she mocked.

"It is actually quite an ingenious idea. This rule was designed to prevent unnecessary verbal abuse or argument between couples. I have to abide by this; I have promised my father."

"Please, tell me the truth, *dear*," she said impatiently.

Chapter 11

"The Oath"

"If the first woman God ever made
was strong enough
to turn the world upside down, all alone,
These women together
ought to be able to turn it back,
and get it right side up again."

—Sojourner Truth

Rahzvon explained to Sophia, "From this point on, any request you have of me, must be presented on paper. I am not to acknowledge any solicitation or inquiry, otherwise."

"I do not understand. Am I to write you a note every time I need you to pass the butter or desire a kiss?" she retorted.

"Now, *you* are being ridiculous. It refers to inquiries of large expenditures and decisions requiring our mutual agreement."

"In other words, I cannot spend my own money?" she asked indignantly and left the divan.

"That is not true, you can purchase—things, small things, stockings and the like."

"This is tyranny!" She plopped down on the window seat.

"Do not be angry with me, Phia. You married a Kosdrevian and I did not make the rules!" he called over to her.

She left the seat and approached him, "Besides, having to beg for your permission to shop, are there other medieval mandatory regulations?" Sophia scoffed.

Rahzvon looked away.

"Look at me! Why are you silent?" she demanded.

He left his seat and walked toward the hearth. "I am sorry, Phia, it is my culture, the manner in which I was raised."

"What are you not telling me, Rahzvon?"

"On the first anniversary of our wedding day, we have to make a *Lourf vomli pronac eoto lourfvomli Pronacteoto.*"

"What in the world is that?"

"A declaration of sorts."

"Oh? Are we are to renew our vows?" Sophia

asked with guarded interest.

"Not exactly; we each have to stand before our families and declare the positive attributes of one another's character."

"That is more like it. That sounds positively romantic; I am looking forward to it." She sighed and sat down in the rocker.

"There is more. That is the day, I must declare your...your character flaws and how I intend to...to correct them," he choked out the words.

She squinted suspiciously. "And then *I* do the same?"

"No—only the husband."

"*Only* the husband?" she repeated and walked toward the hall. "You are going to ridicule me in the presence of my family and then state your prepared punishments?" She turned to leave.

"No punishments! They are called *sedfu nvadi*—complimentary assistance."

"Call them anything you want, Mr. Sierzik. If I am to be insulted, why in the presence of my clan?"

"Knowing this, you shall be inspired to behave more agreeably. The *sedfu ail lus* is to help site and repair any damage in that first year," he said with diplomacy.

"What about the damage for which *you* are responsible?"

"Phia, this is for your benefit, to insure good relations between us."

"Rahzvon, look around. We are not in Kosdrev—we are in Scotland. We can make our own traditions. *No one* shall know if we do not partake in these primeval rituals."

"I would know." He stepped over and looked down on her. "Why should I abandon what I consider to be a good idea?" he asked with conviction. "However, I *will* be presenting you with a gift," he said nonchalantly.

"What? A bull whip?"

"No, something quite nice," he objected.

"Oh, a silver dunce cap that I can don sitting in the corner. No need to worry about the eighteen months, for our first-born—*that* may not be long enough!" She left the room and headed upstairs to simmer.

Rahzvon dropped to the divan and mercilessly scrunched the bolster pillow. "And so it begins," he grumbled. He heard Tavy's voice in the hall.

"Hey, Mrs. Muffet!"

"Do not Mrs. anything me," Sophia denounced. Rahzvon could hear her footsteps as she marched upstairs.

Tavy entered the parlor. "Hope I am not interruptin', Gypsy?" He sat down across from his brooding friend.

"Nothing unusual; another one of her tantrums. How is Trina?"

"Me own personal nursemaid, helpin' tend to me injury." Tavy grinned looking down at his bandaged hand, broken by the thieves who stole the pouch of gems.

"Trina could give Phia some lessons. My wife is so confounded independent. I mention a few innocent traditions and she is up in arms—ready for battle. Granted they are a bit one-sided, but I am not expecting her to wait on me hand and foot. She needs to respect my culture." Rahzvon left the divan with the captive pillow.

"Ye need to respects hers."

Rahzvon swung around. "What is there to respect? She has no significant culture. She may be a Scot but she was not raised as one. *I* know more about Scottish tradition than she."

"That may be true, but she grew up out o' yer country. Ye canna expect and shouldna want her to forget her way o' life. 'Tis only fair."

"McTavish, the Kosdreven traditions are hundreds of years old. I am not about to defy my heritage." He slammed the pillow down to the rocking chair.

"Easy matey. All ye need do is sweeten the pot."

"How?" Rahzvon turned with his hands planted on his hips.

Tavy leaned forward and said quietly, "Inspire her to partake. Dunna demand it. Women dunna take kindly to bein' prodded like cattle. If ye explained the honor of havin' her keep these traditions—yer appreciation, she may be a bit more agreeable."

Rahzvon stared at the rough and tough sailor without speaking. Smiling as one does when waiting for the sunrise at dawn, Tavy watched Rahzvon consider his suggestion. "Ye canna be angry wit' me, Gypsy; ye agree with me. Yer wife requires a great deal of understandin'."

Rahzvon looked to the floor for a moment and then up. "McTavish, coming from any other man, I would not have agreed, but you may be right."

Tavy leaned back. "A wee matter o' give and take. As me dear mother always said, if she wants to sleep wit' the window open, throw on anot'er cover."

Rahzvon nodded in agreement.

"Now, please tell me, is there somethin' yer wee wife desires concernin' her culture?"

Rahzvon's brows knitted objectionably, disturbed by the inquiry.

"Aye, there is."

Tavy grinned. "Out wit' it, man."

Rahzvon closed his eyes with dread.

A half hour later, Sophia was sitting on the edge of the bed and staring out the window. She turned when she heard a knock on the door, followed by Rahzvon's request.

"Phia, may I come in. I have a surprise for you."

"Hmm?" She turned back to the window. "Come in."

Rahzvon entered and stood on the opposite side of the bed. Sophia ignored him.

"Are you not curious as to the gift?" he asked gently.

She offered no reply.

"Please, Phia."

Sophia reluctantly turned, and then made a double take. Her jaw dropped. "Rahzvon, I cannot believe it—you did it! For me!" She stood up on the bed to take in the full view. Rahzvon stood square and tall. "You look so positively handsome! Turn around."

Rahzvon turned slowly in a full circle. "You like it?"

Sophia clasped her hands with delight. "I knew it! I knew that you would look as fine as Uncle Hiram! This is like a dream come true. Whatever made you change your mind?"

"McTavish. These are his. He convinced me that I could not expect you to honor the Kosdreven traditions, if I did not embrace yours."

"Tavy is *so* sweet."

"Hey—I am the one wearing this costume."

Sophia crawled over to the edge of the bed and peered down at his bare knees.

"Excellent," she commented. "But what is this?" She lifted the hemmed edge of the kilt to see the crumpled cotton leg.

"My long underwear—I can only meet you half way on this one," he said uncomfortably.

She withheld her giggles, stood up on the bed, and put her arms around his neck.

"I love you for this." She leaned in and kissed his cheek. "Very well, I shall meet you half way, as well, but I had better be awarded with a great present, if I have to stand before my family."

"Is this not present enough?" He put his hands on her waist.

"For now, but I should think that kissing you in a kilt might be doubly pleasurable."

"As they say, your wish is my command, Mrs. Sierzik."

As the battle ended at the manor, another erupted down the road at Brachney Hall. Hiram's young Uncle Edward and his wife, Naomi, were having a rather heated discussion in their drawing room.

"I do not understand your insistence for returning so quickly," Naomi complained.

"It was supposed to be a *picnic*, Naomi. We *did* comb nearly two-thirds of Duncan Ridge," Edward argued.

"*Only* two-thirds, it may be in the other third."

"*Naomi*, I am not spending another second on this foolishness. I am still on the mend from my fall from the ladder; you cannot expect me to spend hours walking and crawling around the fields."

"I did not ask you to go with me. I could have returned with a servant." She sat down on the rocking chair.

"No, you could not. I shan't have you running off to Duncan Ridge with a servant." He hesitated for a moment, "What would people say?" He took the chair across from her.

"Edward, that is ridiculous! I should go back this very minute and search the other third."

"Are you even sure that it was lost there?"

"I am positive."

"We have devoted enough of our lives searching for it—it is not that important. If it was, you should have taken greater care to keep from losing it."

"Edward, this is not my fault. One does not know when or where an earring will fall off," she defended.

"Then stop wearing them and admire them in your jewel case."

"Very amusing."

Edward turned away, then back. "Why are you staring at me?" He frowned.

"Your neck!" Naomi left her chair to examine it the redness above his collar.

"What is wrong with it?"

"Oh dear me, you received a frightful sunburn."

Edward placed his hand on his neck. "Great Scott! I am on fire!"

"Of course it is hot. Tsk, tsk." She shook her head. "Bad cases always are."

"Well, that is *just* perfect. You know what this means?"

"What?"

"For the next week, my shirt collars will be irritating, which adds to the pain that I am feeling in these knees from crawling over half the countryside!" He rubbed his kneecaps.

"I guess in your pathetic condition, you could stay home and remain in your nightshirt."

Edward threw her an ungrateful smile.

"We will have to go back tomorrow and check the other third; that is all there is to it," Naomi insisted. "You can wear your large-brimmed hat."

"No we are not. I would as soon search for the proverbial needle in the haystack." Edward left his seat. "*Someone* has to face reality and show some common sense."

"Have you no compassion? That is my favorite pair."

"I shall buy you another."

"I do not want another pair; I have had them for years!"

"Where did you get them, anyway?"

Naomi left her rocking chair and did not answer.

"Naomi, I asked a question."

"They are very unusual and I have become accustomed to them. I have never seen another pair like them."

Edward approached her slowly. "*Dearest*, please tell me how you acquired them. I have a right to know; I feel I have spent half my life searching for them."

"One—searching for only one of them."

Naomi glanced to the window when the McDonnally carriage fatefully pulled up in the drive. She jumped at the opportunity to escape her husband's inquisition and rushed to the hall where the butler was greeting the guests.

"Hiram and Livia have come!" Naomi ran to the hall. "Hello, come on into the drawing room," she invited.

"Good morning, Naomi," Livia said, entering in

front of Hiram. "I hope that we are not intruding. We had breakfast with Dagmar at Grimwald. She is doing an excellent job in converting it into the schoolhouse."

"It was so very generous of her to donate it," Naomi said, flashing a welcome smile toward Hiram.

"Naomi," Hiram nodded as they followed her to the parlor where Edward was squinting skeptically at his wife's hasty exit.

"*Edward*, we missed you at the round up. Where have you been?" Hiram sat down on the couch.

"Good morning, and do not ask. Hello, Livia."

"Good morning, Edward." Livia sat down next to Hiram. "We have come to discuss arrangements for a rather late celebration for Rahzvon and Sophia's marriage."

"That is...wonderful," Naomi commented when she noticed Hiram eying Edward's neck.

"You look a wee red, man," Hiram noted.

"A sunburn," Edward grumbled and glanced briefly at Naomi who immediately commented.

"I should ring for tea."

Hiram leaned back into the couch and dropped his hand to the cushion seat where his fingers fell upon a small object. "What do we have here?" He raised it to his face.

Naomi paused in the doorway, turned and went over to see what he was holding.

"My earring! You found it—you wonderful man!" She kissed Hiram's cheek. "Thank you." She put out her hand.

Hiram started to hand it to her when he lifted it closer. "I recognize *this*."

Naomi's smile suddenly disappeared. Edward's eyes narrowed.

Hiram grinned. "This is one of the pair that I brought back from my trip to Wales." He turned it over in his palm, "Yes it was handmade by an old woman, who had a wee cottage on a hill." He looked up at Naomi, now nervously biting her lip. "I remember your face when I..." He stopped, glanced at Edward's discontent expression then to Livia who looked away uncomfortably. He cleared his throat. "Aye, 'twas a long time ago." Hiram placed it in Naomi's hand.

"Excuse me, I will check on the tea," Naomi moved as though wearing blinders in her exit, while Edward stared suspiciously at her vanishing form.

Hiram drew Edward back into the conversation, "Edward, my man, sorry you missed it—the showdown, that is."

"You need not remind me." Peeved, Edward walked to the window.

"Aye, young McTavish's culprits were met by the faithful men of Lochmoor Glen...*save one*," Hiram taunted.

"And the women," Livia added.

Hiram put his arm around Livia's shoulders. "Aye, our fair women—ready to protect their men, armed with a fearsome array of kitchen utensils and the like."

"Do not torment me, Hiram," Edward said with disappointment.

Naturally, Hiram seized the opportunity to poke fun at his sensitive uncle and recounted the capture of Tavy's blackmailers. Edward, being a great fan of the western novel, listened attentively, regretting his absence in the thrilling event.

"'Tis not enough that I missed one of the infrequent adventures in Lochmoor, but today, I was bruising my knees, crawling all over Duncan Ridge, getting sun burnt, looking for an earring that was on the divan!" Edward's face, now, was burning brighter than his sunburn.

Naomi returned. "The tea shall be..." She stopped, seeing her husband's enraged expression. "I think that I shall tell the cook to bring some, um... some tarts, as well." She turned abruptly toward the hall, wishing she had never mentioned the lost earring.

After the in-depth discussion of the planned marriage celebration and the refreshments, Hiram announced, "You will have to excuse us; we need to be getting back. Our little man is waiting. Oh, Edward, I have started reviewing the Garnett contract. I have found nothing to be unacceptable, thus far. Their estimated cost is the best I have seen, but quite detailed. It will be in my desk. Let me know what you think, as soon as possible."

"I will."

Edward and Naomi bid them one last farewell and returned to the drawing room. Naomi quickly retrieved her knitting basket and removed the makings of a half-finished sweater for Kade. Edward sat down on the divan, transfixed by his wife's quick hands alternating back and forth between the knit and purl stitches. She focused on her work, although her capable hands did not require a close eye.

"Naomi?"

"Yes, dear."

"The earrings were a gift from Hiram?" he asked in a calm controlled tone.

"Yes, dear," she replied without looking up.

"Are they so very important to you, that you found it necessary to spend futile hours searching for them?"

"For one, dear, only one. Had I lost both, it would have been hopeless."

"You did not answer my question. Was it worth the hours we spent?"

"Of course not, dear—it was right here in the divan."

"You are skirting the issue, Naomi."

"I am?"

"Yes, dear, you are. Were you frantic about losing the earring because it was a gift from Hiram?"

She put down her knitting. "Speaking of Hiram, why did you not inform me of this plan to capture Tavy's blackmailers?"

"I do not want to talk about Hiram."

"You mentioned him; I did not. I know you are grumpy because of that nasty burn on your neck." She left her chair. "You sit right there and relax. I shall prepare a vinegar compress for it."

Naomi escaped, and Edward, who was confused by the turn of the conversation, was none the wiser about her attachment to the recovered earring.

On the carriage ride to McDonnally Manor, Hiram, too, addressed Livia. "I apologize for mentioning the earrings. I did not intend to make you or Naomi uncomfortable. I merely spoke my first thoughts, surprised in seeing them after twenty years. You do understand?"

"I understand."

Her quick response led Hiram to continue.

"The circumstances of the purchase were so unusual; I naturally was taken aback in seeing one of them. You see, Naomi insisted that I was not to bring back something for her, but when I met this woman, when wandering the hills, I felt the need to purchase them. She was such an excellent silversmith—the woman in the hills. You do understand?"

"Yes, I do."

"I never met a woman silversmith. As you know, I wear very little jewelry and my mother had countless pieces from my father, so, I was compelled to purchase something. When I saw the earrings, I knew immediately that Naomi would adore them. She always had an affinity toward silver; she said gold was ostentatious." He stopped, pondered for a minute, and laughed. "She made me promise to never buy her a gold wedding ban—" Seeing Livia's negative expression, he closed his eyes with regret for his comment. "You understand, do you not, Livy?" he mumbled.

Livia reached over and laid her hand on his. "Yes, I understand. I am certainly glad that you are not one to become unhinged at the slightest information of past, generous gestures."

"Indeed?" he asked cautiously.

"Otherwise, you, like Edward, would have difficulty in learning of such extravagant gifts such as the jewelry, flowers, clothing, furs, diamonds and carriages that I have received," she said looking out the window.

"*Carriages?*" He forced a smile as his jaw tightened.

"You need not worry, Hiram. I tried to return them, but they would not accept them. I donated many of them to charity."

"Another good reason why I chose you."

"I miss the baby, Hiram."

He enclosed his hands around hers and studied her innocent face. *Aye and a fine mother, as well.*

Chapter 111

"A Man's home..."

"I have a garden of my own,
Shining with flow'rs of ev'ry hue;
I loved it dearly while alone,
But I shall love it more with you:"

—Thomas Moore

Another difference of opinion emerged in the garden at Hiram's estate. Beatrice, Naomi's mother, and Daniel, Hiram's dear friend, sat quietly staring at one another. Their prior discussion of rebuilding Daniel's bookstore, which had been lost to arson, had ended when Daniel mentioned his desire to construct it in his birthplace, Dublin. At this point, Beatrice came to the realization that, although she loved Daniel, moving to Ireland was not at all desirable; her family members resided in Scotland and London.

"Birdie, I mentioned Dublin because I was thinkin' we should start fresh—away from London and Lochmoor Glen. Ya were married to Nat'an here."

"I understand Daniel. Yes, I agree that I need to start a new life, but I have already spent so many years away from Jeremiah and Naomi."

"Jeremiah is travelin' most of the time and we can visit Naomi as often as ya like."

"That is very generous of you, but not very realistic. There will be entirely too much time needed in organizing the shop and promoting business. I shan't go to Lochmoor Glen without you and you cannot leave the shop for many months, once it is erected."

"Birdie, a shop such as mine could not support us wit' the wee business I would draw here in Lochmoor Glen."

"I know."

"Is there anything that ya would like to be doin' besides runnin' the shop wit' me?"

"Well, yes. I always had a secret desire to have my own tailor shop. Nothing very big; just room enough for a good machine and a cutting table... perhaps, a few storage shelves."

"Aye? Well, I hae an idea. What would ya say to combinin' our efforts?"

"How so?"

"Instead of buildin' a shop as large as me first, what would ya say to creatin' a combination shop wit' nooks? A tailorin' shop for you, a small book corner, and a toy store."

"A toy store?"

"Aye, Dagmar's store has only a couple recipe books and but a few toys."

"You want to build it here in Lochmoor Glen?" Beatrice asked, grinning.

"We agreed to start fresh and I canna think o' a better way than to shrink and expand."

Beatrice laughed. "Are you certain? Do you really think we can drum up enough business?"

"Wit' the Saturday puppet shows we will be the talk o' the village. This way, ya need not disappoint Hiram wit' his plans to build yer cottage."

"Puppet shows? My cottage?"

"I might be convinced to share me shop, if ya share yer cottage."

"Hiram is an extraordinary man."

"None finer."

"Oh, I can think of one." Beatrice smiled.

When Hiram and Livia returned to the manor, Livia went off to care for the baby while Hiram tended to a nearly forgotten business transaction. Three quarters of an hour later, Hiram left his study. He entered the parlor where, once again, Kade was exercising his lungs. Hiram found Eloise rocking the baby, attempting to console him with a little German ditty.

Hiram then broke into song, creating an unlikely duet. Kade immediately turned toward him and stopped crying. Hiram ended the phrase.

Hiram lifted the baby from Eloise's weary arms. "You are being belligerent again, eh, Master Kade?" he asked.

"Sorry, sir. He favors only you."

"I apologize for his poor manners. Where is Miss Nichols?"

"She was unsuccessful with the baby and left to the west wing, I believe, sir."

"Come along, lad. Let us track down your mother."

"Sir, I know that it is not my place to say anything, but Miss Nichols left in a frightful state."

"Aye?"

"Yes, sir, she was very disappointed and frustrated that the baby did not take to her. I thought you should know of this."

"I appreciate your concern. Thank you, Eloise."

"Shall I wait tea, sir?"

"Aye, I will ring for it."

"Yes, sir."

Hiram carried Kade down the corridors pointing out the ancestral portraits to his future heir. Hiram entered the conservatory where Livia was admiring the harpsichord.

"Here is your mother, Kade. Is she not the most beautiful woman in the world?"

"This is quite lovely," Livia said sullenly, not taking her focus from the musical instrument.

"It has been in our family for many years. Mother played it quite often while my father was away. She taught me. Shall I play for you?" He started to hand Kade to her.

"No." She walked over to the window, shelving about a dozen potted plants. "This is quite nice."

"My mother was always saddened by the

coming of winter and the garden dying out. Father had the shelved window installed to provide her with a winter garden. Eloise did her best to restore it."

"Thoughtful man. He must have loved her dearly."

"Or he was driven by his guilt for her loneliness," Hiram said disdainfully. "Livy, I thought we would go for an outing today. We can take the new pram and give Kade his first ride."

"You can go, I have to prepare my list for the day school," she said stroking the heart-shaped leaf of the pothos plant.

"That will never do. I have so little free time. Kade and I want you to come along. We may get lost," he teased.

"I said, I *cannot*, Hiram!"

Hiram, initially shocked by her outburst, paused, then said sternly, "Stand right there. Do not move until I return."

Hiram carried the baby to the kitchen and took the warm bottle from the pan. He checked the temperature on his wrist, gave it to Kade, and handed him to Eloise.

A few minutes later, Hiram returned to the conservatory. He walked directly over to Livia, placed his hands on her shoulders and turned her around. Livia looked up warily. He addressed her, withholding his anger.

"I know that you are frustrated with the baby, but do not *ever* shout at me again."

Livia's eyes immediately filled with tears that trickled down her cheeks. The disarming reaction gave him cause to step back and unhand her.

"You women—why is it that every time I try to take a stand, you all fall to tears? This is not fair—you know that I cannot deal with this." He ran his

hand across his beard and began pacing. Livia never
moved, but sobbed openly.

"Livy, I demand that you stop."

Livia tried, but now whimpered pitifully like a
small child afraid to cry for fear of being beaten.
Hiram shook his head in frustration and hurried
over to confront her.

Instead he comforted her. "Now, now." He
embraced her and stroked her hair. "Please do not
cry. Come, talk with me." He guided her over to the
bench at the harpsichord and sat her down next to
him. They sat for a minute or two until her sobbing
resided.

"Livy, Kade behaves with me because he
senses that I am in-charge—the master of the
house."

"Begging your pardon, but that is the silliest
reasoning I have ever heard. He simply wants you
and no one else. It does not surprise me; everyone is
attracted to you," she said spitefully.

"Do you blame me for this? Do you think that
I secretly conspire with the lad to cry when you hold
him?"

"Of course not. The fact is that I am not part of
his life and shan't ever be. You shall have to find him
a new mother—one he prefers." She left the bench.

"*Now*, who is being silly? Livy, it is a phase. I
am certain of it. He was traumatized when he lost
his mother. I was the first to pick him up after the
accident. The same thing happened with Ludwig."

She turned to him. "Beethoven?"

"No, Ludwig—my duck—my childhood pet."

"You are comparing Kade to a duck?" she said
skeptically.

"Aye. A dog killed Ludwig's mother when he
was a duckling. I rescued him and he followed me

around from that day on."

"That may be the case, but that does not change anything. I feel that I need to leave for awhile." She looked to the floor.

"Leave? Where would you go, Livy?" he asked sympathetically.

"Anywhere."

Hiram followed her to the window. "Love, running away *again* is not the solution. Give Kade another chance. Come walk with us after tea. He needs time to adjust. We all do. The three of us need time alone together. We are a family, now."

Livia wanted this bond as much as Hiram, but could not imagine how she could convince Kade that she could be the perfect mother. She looked hopelessly up at Hiram, tucked her arm under his, and went with him to the dining room to give it yet another try.

After tea, Eloise outfitted the pram with an extra bottle and blankets.

"Thank you, Eloise," Hiram said placing Kade into the buggy and helping Livia with her wrap. Livia cautiously tucked the blanket around the little passenger before Hiram carried the baby carriage down the steps from the portal. The hopeful little family headed down the road toward the Dugan cottage.

Hiram suggested that Livia push the carriage, but during her attempt, Kade gave an objectionable cry. Hiram resumed his position at the helm.

Harriet Dugan met them in front of her home. "Afternoon, Mr. McDonnally, Miss Nichols! Ye hae the wee one wit' ye, I see."

"Aye, tis a bonnie day for a stroll. Where is your fine husband? I need to speak with him," Hiram asked.

"He's around back oilin' the harness," Harriet explained, pointing toward the shed.

"Excuse me, ladies," Hiram said abandoning the carriage.

"But, Hiram," Livia panicked, as Kade began to cry in discovering Hiram's absence. "He is very attached to Hiram!" Livia explained to Harriet over the cries.

Hiram ignored Kade's wails and kept walking. Harriet moved in and removed the upset child from the carriage. She tried patting, bouncing and singing. Kade's cries grew louder.

Out of frustration and desperation, Harriet handed Kade to the objecting mother.

"Ye better take him, Miss, he wants his mama."

"No, I—"

Harriet placed the squealing baby in Livia's arms.

To Livia's shock, Kade stopped crying and stared up at her. Livia looked to Mrs. Dugan in astonishment.

"Aye. Ye are his mother now. He needs ye."

Hiram watched with pleasure as Livia smiled holding the calm infant. Hiram's scheme had resolved the problem; his assumption that Kade would turn to the one most familiar and closest to him in his absence, was correct. Hiram returned to the happy scene, concealing his satisfaction.

"Look, darling, he is quite content, now," Livia said, beaming."

"Aye, Livy, 'twas a brief phase." He turned to Harriet. "Tell Joseph that I shall speak with him later."

"Aye, hae a pleasant walk."

"Thank you," Hiram said while Livia stood in awe at the smiling infant.

"Shall I put him back in the pram, Livy?"

"No, Hiram. My son wants me to carry him for awhile."

Hiram was quite content to push the empty pram for the next half hour and Livia was equally happy to carry Kade, despite her aching arms.

The other loving couple at the manor, Rahzvon and Sophia sat in the parlor, cuddling on the window seat.

"Phia, we need to find a place to live."

"We have a place to live—right here."

"We are not staying here. We need a small house—a home to return to, when we begin traveling. Gaelon is sending me to Brussels next week."

Sophia swiveled toward him. "Why did you not tell me? That gives me so little time to prepare."

"I only learned of it an hour ago. He put everything on hold due to the difficulty with Tavy."

"I highly doubt that was the only reason your brother has chosen to remain here," Sophia commented, observing her mother and Gaelon conversing next to the east fountain.

"Yes, you McDonnally women are the Sierzik Achilles heel. Come along, we should go to Ambersway. There is a small cottage there for sale."

"A *small* cottage? Is there such a thing as a large cottage?"

Sophia ordered one of the McDonnally carriages. An hour later, she and Rahzvon arrived at the property.

"This is a house for *people*?" Sophia stared

wide-eyed at the minute stone building. Rahzvon hopped down and offered her a hand, which she refused.

"What are you doing?" he asked.

"We are not going in there, are we?" Sophia asked, crinkling her nose.

"Yes, we are. I think it has possibilities."

"For what?"

Rahzvon shook his head and thrust his hand toward her.

Sophia scowled, took it, and climbed down from the carriage. "Rahzvon, how am I to step on these flagstones? There are thistles everywhere."

"You had no difficulty traversing the terrain in Kosdrev and it was much worse."

"I wore my ugly boots, there," she said, awkwardly contorting her body with each step. "This is absurd," she muttered when they reached the door.

"Look there," he pointed to a vacant spot on the step, "a place where you can store your ugly boots. They will be ready each time you leave." He threw her a teasing grin.

Sophia barely had time to roll her eyes before Rahzvon opened the door and dragged her inside.

"Yes, it definitely has possibilities," he said eyeing the sturdy walls.

"This is not a house, this is a *bothy*. Uncle Edward's tool shed is larger."

"It is small, but make note—it will take very little effort for you to keep it clean."

"Clean? Who is going to clean?" Sophia ran her finger across the dusty table and stuck out her tongue in disgust.

"Well, I certainly am not," he said calmly, examining the window frame.

"There is only one room, Rahzvon. Where shall the maid live?"

"In some household that can actually afford her."

"You cannot be serious about living here."

"I can. All it needs is a coat of paint and a few furnishings."

Sophia turned with her hands on her hips, "We absolutely cannot live here. There is no stove or even a place for one."

"We do not need a stove. In my country there are no stoves; cooking is done over the hearth."

"Mr. Sierzik, this is the twentieth century. I am not living like a caveman—cavewoman! Why, this is smaller than a cave! The cave people lived better than this."

"Phia, stop complaining. We need a small home; then we won't have to hire a caretaker to look after it while we are traveling. Someone may move in while we're gone, though," he commented, tapping on the rickety, wooden table.

"No self-respecting rat would take up residence here. This room is not much larger than the maid's room off the manor kitchen."

"*Phia,*" he faced her, "we are not spending a lot of time here and it is better than the inn."

"It is not! It is dirty and disgusting."

"You complained that the rooms at the inn were dirty."

She folded her hands and held them tightly at her chest. "It is in the middle of nowhere."

"Exactly. Away from *everyone.*"

"I do not want to be isolated from human life." She shoved the wooden chair under the table.

"We are not returning to your uncle's each time that we have a holiday...I want privacy." He reached over and drew his finger across her cheek.

She pulled away. "You are daft! I would sooner live in the dungeon at Kosdrev than here! At least there would be room for both of us to stand at the same time."

"*This* subject is closed for discussion. If you have a better suggestion, present it to me in writing." He pushed passed her, through the door.

She yelled, chasing after him, "I do not need paper to tell you that we are staying at my uncle's!"

Rahzvon swung around, "Did you hear what you said? 'My uncle's. McDonnally Manor—Hiram's— and it is for McDonnallys. I want my own castle for *my* family." He climbed into the carriage.

"Castle? I have made sand castles larger than this. And the only family small enough to raise here would be mice, which I am certain the rats would kill for invading their territory!" she shouted, as he helped her to her seat.

"I have heard enough. I am going to find furniture for it tomorrow after I sign the purchase papers."

"Furniture?" Sophia scoffed. "Who needs it? We can bring two pillows from my bed to use as mattresses and a cigar box for our children to sleep in."

"Your insolence and ungrateful attitude appalls me, Phia. I try to find us our first home and *this* is the way you behave. Look at it." He pointed to the cottage. "All it needs is a little attention. You are spoiled. Ever since you came to live with Hiram, you expect only the best of everything. Well, I may have a decent income now, but we shan't squander it away on unnecessary frivolities."

"Such as a wooden floor, as opposed to dirt? Buy me a shovel for our first anniversary and I shall keep our lovely little home in tip-top shape!" She folded her arms in a huff. Rahzvon glared at her and tapped on the roof for the driver to move on.

When they returned to McDonnally Manor, Sophia stormed inside with Rahzvon trailing her. She entered the parlor and plopped down on the divan.

He stood over her, hands at his hips breathing hard with frustration. "If you want to live here, you may. But when we return from Belgium, *I* shall stay at the inn." When he turned to leave his pouting wife, he nearly ran over Hannah standing in the doorway. "Excuse me."

Hannah moved aside and went to sit next to her daughter. "A problem, Sophia?"

"My husband plans to lock me up in a castle the size of a pantry."

Hannah squinted with confusion.

"Mother, he took me to see this pathetic, tiny rat-trap and is determined to make it his *castle*! It is a quarter the size of this room! I should have brought Uncle Edward's magnifying lens to get a better view."

"Sophia, I am sure that you are exaggerating. A man needs to provide a home for his family."

"A home—not a *shed*."

"I do not know Rahzvon very well. However, it is obvious that he loves you dearly, and means you no harm. He risked his life to reclaim his inheritance, so that he could marry you. He may be frugal, but you cannot deny him his right to his independence."

"Not you, too? Gaelon has influenced you, has he not? What about me? My rights to a nice home?"

"Some of the wealthiest people in the world reside in breath-taking elaborate mansions, such as this, but are frightfully discontent because they are absent of love. You, my daughter, could be happy in a one room flat with Rahzvon, if you would remember that it is not the walls that make a home—it is the love within them."

Sophia sat silent. Her mother had never spoken with such frankness, or so profoundly on the subject of love.

"Sophia, I dream of a life such as Rahzvon offers you—a small house that I could furnish and repair with someone who loved me. Reconsider, Sophia; you have it all."

Hannah patted her daughter's hand and left her to ponder her suggestion.

Several minutes later Sophia found Rahzvon leaning on the garden gate watching the horses in the pasture. He glanced over his shoulder toward Sophia, but said nothing.

"May I go with you to choose the furniture?" she asked meekly. "Or do I need to make that request in writing?"

Rahzvon turned, placed his arm over her shoulders, and pulled her next to him. He continued watching the horses.

Chapter IV

"Mr. Alburnett"

"Little deeds of kindness,
Little words of love,
Make our earth an Eden
Like the heaven above."

—Julia Fletcher Carney

That afternoon Rahzvon and Sophia summoned a coachman to take them on the scenic route to the home of "Old Man" Alburnett, a fine woodworker and dedicated craftsman. Joseph Dugan had recommended his shop as a source for Rahzvon and Sophia's furniture search. The shop was an extension of the barn located on a farm near Ambersway—not far from Rahzvon and Sophia's new home.

The driver placed the basket lunch that Eloise had prepared, into the carriage and helped Sophia to the seat next to Rahzvon.

After they had passed through the village, Sophia withdrew a slip of paper from her handbag and handed it to Rahzvon.

"What is this?" he asked.

"My furniture requests; the law *does* require that I submit them through correspondence."

Rahzvon chuckled. "Indeed." He drew an inquisitive expression and read them. "Are you certain that you need this? I thought my braiding before we retired was enough to insure your beauty," he teased.

"Darling, I need a looking glass to admire the product of your efforts."

"True. I am becoming quite the artisan with my hair creations. How did you like the two braids that I deigned last night?" he asked proudly.

"The antlers?"

"You are the one who was too lazy to sit up while I braided them."

"I was not being lazy; I was tired."

"Lately, you are tired all the time. If I did not know better, I would think that you were not eating enough to sustain you through the day. Maybe you are eating too much. That can make you tired—like the pigs."

"Like the pigs?" she took offense.

"Certainly. They go to sleep after they eat."

Sophia immediately moved to the opposite side of the carriage.

Rahzvon grinned as she sat in her normal pouting state. But then, something happened which he did not expect—she burst into tears.

"Phia?" he said tenderly and moved over next to her. "I was not comparing you to a pig," he pleaded. "It was all in jest. Please stop crying."

She took her handkerchief from her handbag and wiped her eyes. "You are not attracted to me anymore. You think that I resemble a pig," she said pathetically.

"No, I think no such thing. And, yes, I am attracted to you and I always will be. You are my life, Phia."

"Then tell me—you never tell me."

"Tell you what?"

"Please, tell me that I am beautiful."

"Oh *Phia* you *are,* my beautiful, little one." He took her hand. "You cannot imagine the thoughts that were running through my head that night I first arrived in Lochmoor Glen. When I saw you standing in front of the house and you looked at me—I wanted to jump down from the cart and take you in my arms."

"*Rahzvon,* honestly?"

"Yes, I was a rogue taken by the likes of a beautiful woman."

"I thought you incredibly handsome, as well. In fact, I distinctly remember thinking that you were nearly as handsome as my uncle Hiram."

"Nearly, eh?"

"Now, more so." She laid her head against him.

When they arrived at Mr. Alburnett's home, Rahzvon and Sophia left the carriage when they saw an elderly man moving beyond the open barn door. They passed a peculiar row of about a dozen bowls and plates sitting along the drive. All contained remnants of some unknown foodstuffs at various stages of decomposition.

"Hello, sir!" Rahzvon called. The man did not respond.

"Hello!" Sophia called. Still no response. "Perhaps he is deaf."

They went inside. A display of the carpenter's fine work covered the barn floor and walls.

"Sir?" Rahzvon addressed Mr. Alburnett again. He finally turned.

"Good day, miss, lad."

"We have come to purchase some of your furniture. Joseph Dugan suggested that we visit your shop," Rahzvon explained.

"Who? Please, tell me, again. I am hard of hearin'."

Rahzvon increased his volume, "Joseph Dugan."

"Aye, Joe—a good man he is."

"I am Rahzvon Sierzik and this is my wife Sophia."

"Nice to meet the two o' ye." He nodded. "Sierzik? Yer not from these parts."

"No, I am from a small country called—"

"What are ye interested in—tables, chairs?"

"We would like to see your dressing tables!" Sophia interjected.

"Follow me." He led them to a far corner at the back of the barn. "I shall leave ye to look. I hae to feed me hound."

Rahzvon and Sophia looked curiously at one

another. There was not a single dog in view, but they observed Mr. Alburnett place yet another filled bowl in the line along the drive. They shrugged and began inspecting the furniture.

"Look at this one, Phia. It has a huge mirror."

Sophia was busy studying another piece and made no reply.

"Or this one, it has four drawers," he said pulling out the expertly designed, dovetailed connections. His comments went unnoticed.

"This one is small, but quite attractive it has carved—" Rahzvon said turning to see the source of her preoccupation. *Oh, no,* he thought.

There it was. Nothing like he had ever seen in his life. He stepped slowly over to his wife. "Phia, I want to show you a dressing table, over here. It is beautifully veneered." He motioned weakly with his hand.

"No need for that, this is the one I want. Is it not positively perfect?"

"Phia, it is monstrous."

"Granted, it is larger than the usual dressing table, but that is because it has the wardrobe and side table connected to it. And look at this—a full-length looking glass at the end with a little landing. Have you ever seen such carpentry? Every inch is exquisite. I am so happy that you brought me here."

"Everything the man has made is extraordinary. This is grand, but much too large for the cottage."

"No it is not. It shall fit on the wall on the left side when you enter the door," she said admiring the glass drawer pulls.

"That is the only available wall for the bed. Remember, the other had the hearth and the back wall had the door?"

"That is all right. We can put the bed in the middle of the room."

"But that is where the table sits and this would cover the only window."

"We do not need a window. The looking glass will make the room appear larger and open. Eloise always says 'the more mirrors, the more space'."

"*Phia*, please look at the smaller ones. They have looking glasses." He walked over to the larger of the other two pieces. "See this one; it has four drawers."

"This one has eight *and* a wardrobe. Dear, a woman needs drawer space."

"A man needs space to *walk*."

Sophia turned with an indignant look. "You wanted the *little* cottage. I finally agreed. Now, are you suggesting that I have to settle for one of those little girl dressing tables, as well?"

She turned back and stepped up onto the small platform facing the mirror.

"There will be no room for the bed if we purchase this," he said tightening his fists.

"We do not need one."

"Don't need one? Of course we do. Do you expect us to stand to sleep, like horses?"

"Please lower your voice. We do not want Mr. Alburnett to think that we are common peasants. It is very simple; we can roll up blankets, store them in the wardrobe, and sleep on the floor.

"Sleep on the floor?" Rahzvon raised his voice, again. "I have slept on the barn floor for months. I am a man of means, now. I am not going to go through life without a bed!"

Sophia stood in front of the looking glass. Rahzvon watched her as she started to quiver. He raised a brow as he heard whimpers. He moved to the side of the mirror to focus on her likeness. Tears were streaming down her face. He could not believe it.

"All right, Phia. It is yours. We will fit it in...some way."

She turned around sobbing and stepped down. He embraced her, confused by yet another one of her emotional outbreaks.

After Rahzvon paid for the mammoth dressing table, looking glass, wardrobe combination, he inquired about arrangements to have it delivered.

"Ye must have a mighty large bedroom for this piece," Mr. Alburnett commented walking them to the carriage. Sophia smiled.

"Need anythin' else?" he asked.

"No, that is all we have room for," Rahzvon explained through clenched teeth.

In passing the line of bowls, Sophia asked, "Sir, do you have a lot of dogs?"

"Nay," he shook his head. "Only one."

Rahzvon and Sophia glanced curiously at one another.

"I did not see him," Sophia commented.

"He disappeared twelve days ago, but he shall come back. I have fresh food waitin' every day."

Sophia nodded as the coachman helped her into the carriage. Rahzvon bid Mr. Alburnett farewell and joined Sophia. As the carriage pulled away, Sophia began to cry, again.

"Now, what is wrong? Is there something else you wanted? Please tell me that you have not changed your mind."

"No." She sniffed and wiped her eyes. "I fear that his dog is not returning."

Rahzvon put his arm around her knowing that she was probably right, but he could offer no words of consolation. He instructed the coachman to stop the carriage at the livery in Ambersway.

When they arrived, Rahzvon climbed out. "Phia, wait here, I have to talk to someone about delivering the furniture."

In his absence, Sophia, feeling melancholy about the carpenter's loss, stared teary-eyed out the window. She watched a group of children huddled around something of interest. A boy of about seven years of age and a smaller girl of similar features, turned, holding a tiny pup. Sophia straightened and wiped her eyes. Another little boy sat with a puppy on the ground between his legs. Sophia moved quickly across the seat, left the carriage, and hurried over to the children.

"Excuse me. Which of you owns these puppies?"

"They're mine," a tall, thin girl of about twelve years of age, replied.

"Are they for sale?" Sophia asked.

"No, Mum."

"Oh." Disheartened, Sophia turned to leave.

"Do ye want one, Mum?" the girl called.

Sophia spun around. "Not for myself—for a gift."

"Ye can hae one. Me father says, I hae to find homes for 'em. We canna keep 'em. All are promised but this one," she held up the little black and white ball of fluff.

"I shall take it. I am giving it to Mr. Alburnett, down the road. Do you know him?"

"Aye. He would be needin' a dog. Me father says a stranger came through and stole his. I canna remember; that was many years ago. I was but six."

He has been waiting nearly six years. Sophia's eyes welled up. "How awful; we shall deliver it to him, as soon as my husband is finished at the livery."

"Is he yer husband?" The girl pointed at Rahzvon coming out of the livery.

"Yes, that is him."

The girl sighed. "I pray that me husband is as bonnie," she said in a dazed state, staring at Rahzvon as he approached. This brought a much needed smile to Sophia's face, as she was about to fall to pieces, again.

"What have we here?" Rahzvon asked fearfully. *Not a dog, too.*

"Mr. Alburnett's newest family member." Sophia held up the little wriggling pup.

When the carriage reached the lane leading to the carpenter's barn, Rahzvon lifted the puppy from Sophia's lap and carried it a short distance. When he released it, it made a beeline for the bowls. Rahzvon comforted Sophia as she wept watching Mr. Alburnett playing with the little dog, as they drove away. Rahzvon rolled his eyes wondering how he was ever to cope with such an uncommonly, overly-sensitive wife.

A few days later, Sophia's pride-and-joy was to be delivered to the cottage. While waiting for its arrival, Sophia surveyed the situation.

"I think that some cute curtains and a nice rug will help, immensely. I cannot thank you enough for having the floor installed, my love."

"Sitting your dressing table extraordinaire in the dirt was not an option and it certainly did not take long," Rahzvon said, sitting cross-legged on the new floor.

"Yes, I think a quiet green fabric for the

window."

"No one will see it. The window will be covered with your mirror."

"Oh, I forgot. Well, that is more money we can save."

He held his tongue, having paid an exorbitant amount for her vanity set.

Four men arrived shortly with a wagon carrying the furniture piece. Under Rahzvon's instruction, they placed it on the only available wall, received their tip, and left the couple in a state of awe.

"It seems so much larger in here," Sophia commented, trying to smile.

"It was in a building thirty feet high; it would naturally appear smaller there."

"You do not think it is ostentatious, do you?" she asked.

"It is what you want. That is all that matters. However, we should separate the pieces."

"Absolutely not! How could you suggest such a thing?" She stepped upon the platform and smiled at her reflection. "Rahzvon, where are you going to keep your clothing?"

Assuming that he would be entitled to at least one drawer, he paused to reconsider. "I guess, in my satchel hanging on that hook," he pointed to the metal hook on the backdoor.

"Oh." Sophia puffed out her cheeks, and then sighed. "I was going to hang my coats there...but you can have it. Darling, I can hardly wait to show everyone. Let's invite them this afternoon!"

Rahzvon conveniently turned to examine the metal hook to hide his disapproval. "Whatever you want, Phia," he surrendered.

***

Later that afternoon, all of the local relatives accepted the invitation. However, due to the lack of available space in their new home, Rahzvon convinced Sophia to invite only a few at a time. She agreed in part, but did not want to slight either her mother or uncle, so she invited Hannah and Gaelon with Hiram, Livia, and Kade to be their first guests.

When the McDonnally carriage arrived, Sophia ran out to greet it; Rahzvon sat solemnly on a wooden chair on the small porch. With little enthusiasm, he stood at the sight of the emerging guests.

"Welcome everyone!" Sophia said bubbling with pride for her new residence. She ran up to Hiram carrying Kade. "Hello, my sweet baby." She kissed his tiny hand.

Hiram locked eyes with Rahzvon. "Mr. Sierzik." Hiram raised a questioning brow at the sight of the tiny abode.

"Hiram." Rahzvon smiled at Kade and opened the door. Rahzvon then closed his eyes for a second, anticipating the worst. The three couples squeezed inside.

"Here it is mother, Livia. Is it not the most beautiful combination you have ever seen?"

"It is beautiful. Quite large, but definitely beautiful," Hannah replied, eying the enormous wardrobe.

"Very unique, Sophia," Livia commented, forcing a smile, as she tried to see around the other guests.

Sophia lined up everyone in two rows, with the taller in the back. There was no room to spare. She started her tour, beginning with the locking drawers and ending with the compartmental vanity, next to the mirror and platform.

Hiram leaned toward Rahzvon, "Please, tell me that you did not actually agree to this."

"I had no choice."

"Every man has a choice." He looked down at Kade. "Remember that, son."

Gaelon watched cautiously when his brother's aggressive frown appeared. He swallowed when Rahzvon replied, "Please, step outside with me, Hiram."

"Livy, please take Kade."

"But Hiram—"

"Please, Livy."

Hiram lifted Kade over Sophia's head, down to Livia. Gaelon looked protectively toward Rahzvon as the two men squeezed by to leave the cottage.

"I said I had no choice because your niece was crying like a baby," Rahzvon explained.

"Sophia, crying? A tantrum I can imagine, but tears? What did you say to her?" Hiram demanded.

"Nothing, nothing at all. She cries all the time," Rahzvon took offense.

"She is obviously not happy with the marriage." Hiram folded his arms across his chest.

"Now, wait a minute. You saw her, she is ecstatic about her...her dressing table thing and the house."

"House?" Hiram looked skeptically at the cottage.

"For now, it is fine. We will be traveling most of the time."

"Aye, Gaelon mentioned that. It is for the best. I cannot imagine the two of you with your tempers in these close quarters."

"Yes, the McDonnally temperament normally requires a place as large as yours," Rahzvon said pointedly.

"Touché, Mr. Sierzik. Shall we go back in—if physically possible?"

Rahzvon reluctantly led the way.

When they returned, Gaelon asked, "Rahzvon, where are you going to put the bed?"

Rahzvon glanced uncomfortably toward Hiram, "We do not have one. We are sleeping on the floor. It was Phia's idea."

Sophia smiled. Hiram looked to Livia who stared blankly, refusing to express any opinion on the matter.

"Where?" Gaelon asked studying the floor space the couples occupied.

Rahzvon did not answer. Hiram looked around the room then noted something strange on the ceiling, lurking nearly three feet above them. "What is that?" he asked.

Rahzvon looked uncomfortably away.

Sophia overheard her uncle's inquiry, "That is our pulley system. It was also my idea." She lifted the slotted basket of fruit revealing a hook in the center of the table. "You see when it is time to retire, we simply hoist the table to the ceiling, to give space for our bed rolls."

"What about the chairs, Sophia?" Hannah asked.

"Oh, we sit them outside on the porch."

"Oh." Her mother pursed her lips and looked uneasily toward her brother.

Sophia continued, "We do have to mind our heads, so as not to bump them on the table legs. I should like them to be made to fold up someday."

"Are you not afraid that it may fall on you?" Livia asked.

"Not at all. My protective husband added an extra safety chain."

It was all Hiram could do to withhold his laughter.

"Now, ladies, let me show you our private bath facility," Sophia announced proudly.

"Hiram, could you please take Kade?" Livia asked.

"Aye, Love."

After a bit of creative maneuvering of the crowd of seven, Hiram cradled Kade in his arms. Sophia led the women through the back door and squeezed them into a small addition providing a claw-footed tub and outhouse facilities.

"We did not know it was here when we bought our home. We thought it was the backdoor!" Sophia laughed. "Of course it is in dire need of repair, but it has possibilities, do you not think?"

Livia and Hannah reserved their honest opinions for a later date and nodded.

Gaelon looked at the pulley. "Ingenious."

"Aye, very clever," Hiram agreed. "Perhaps you could install some more to hoist up a divan and a couple of easy chairs and lower them as needed," Hiram laughed.

Sophia stood in the doorway. Feeling insulted and reduced to tears, she fled through the door.

Chapter V

"Expectations"

"Some old things are lovely
Warm still with life of forgotten men
who made them."

—David H. Lawrence

Rahzvon turned to the guilty uncle. "You *see?*" he said sharply, and then left to chase after his wife.

Livia and Hannah shook their heads hopelessly at Hiram who stood wearing a look of pure innocence. Rahzvon caught up with Sophia who was sitting on a log and sat down next to her.

"Remember when we sat in the woods together for the first time? You had Rusty with you," Rahzvon said gently.

Sophia slowly looked toward him. "You want to buy me a dog?" she sniffled.

Rahzvon's eyes widened. N*ow what have I done?* He could not answer negatively for fear of the results. He put his arm around her and gulped.

A minute later Sophia was shouting with delight as she greeted her guests who were preparing to leave. "My wonderful husband is getting me a dog!"

Hiram looked toward Rahzvon, tightened his lips, and shook his head. Rahzvon's eyes narrowed.

Before they embarked to return to McDonnally Manor, Livia gave Hiram an encouraging nudge to address the newlyweds.

Hiram cleared his throat. "I realize that you chose to marry without notifying us—your family—but I will ignore that for the time being."

Rahzvon and Sophia listened curiously.

"However," Hiram continued, "the family has decided that it is time to formally announce this marriage. Livy, Naomi, Edward and I would like to host a celebration. As we are still waiting for the arrival of Kade's christening gown, that celebration is delayed; we are making preparation for yours."

"A party?" Sophia asked, glowing with excitement. This reaction came as no surprise to anyone, for all were aware that Sophia lived for social gatherings...and food. She gratefully embraced Hiram, and then the other hosts.

"Thank you." Rahzvon mustered up a smile. He was content to be accepted into the McDonnally clan, but relieved that Sophia was, officially, a cottage-dwelling Sierzik.

Over the next few days, Rahzvon looked forward to the celebration, despite Sophia's many attempts to include him in the final decorating decisions. It was not long before wedding gifts began arriving at the manor from all corners of the world. Sophia insisted that they open them before the party. No one dare oppose her desire. Rahzvon was by no means ignorant in his understanding of the social position of the clan, but he found the number and extravagance of the gifts to be unfathomable.

That memorable evening, the honored couple sat in the parlor, lost in a sea of gift-wrap and brown paper. Crates and boxes flowed out into the hall. There was barely room for the audience, which included Guillaume and his parents, Tavy and Trina, and the local McDonnally family members. All regarded the bride as she opened the gifts.

Sophia studied the new vacuum cleaner, "Well, it is remarkable, but I shan't need this Baby Daisy—my housemaid will, though." Rahzvon raised a disapproving brow and sat it next to the bean slicer from Miss Nettlepin and the hand-wringer washing machine from Hiram's accountant.

Trina picked up a rather large box sitting next to her and gave it to Sophia. "Open this, next!"

Sophia read the label, "It is from the Netherlands."

"Friends of mine," Hiram confirmed.

Sophia carefully removed the excelsior, "Oh

my. Look, Rahzvon."

"Unbelievable."

Sophia lifted the carved ivory and walnut statue of the Lamentation.

"It is glorious and the note says that it is over one-hundred and fifty years old," Sophia said in awe. "Poor elephant who gave his life for this, I guess it is an honor though—being a statue of Jesus and all." While observing the grieving scene over Christ's death, everyone pondered the irony of Sophia's concern for the sacrificial elephant. They then nodded in agreement.

The well-meaning Guillaume left his seat immediately. "Over one-hundred years old? I had better put it over on the table where it will be safe."

"No!" everyone shouted, fearing for the piece.

While Guillaume returned to his seat, trying to regain his dignity, Rahzvon carried the art-piece to the safety of the mantle.

Next, Albert and Edward moved a large crate over to Sophia. Rahzvon rolled his eyes. *Where are we going to put all of this? I will have to build a storage shed bigger than the cottage.*

"I removed the side," Albert said, returning to his seat beside Eloise.

"It is from Edward, Allison, and I," Naomi said while Sophia quickly pulled away the packing and gasped at the beautiful bureau.

Eloise put her hand to her mouth and mumbled, "A Dresden from Germany."

Naomi explained, "We thought perhaps, Rahzvon could use a place for his clothing."

"Yes, Darling, now you need not use your satchel." Sophia rubbed the back of Rahzvon's hand.

Everyone laughed.

"We thank you. It is exquisite," Rahzvon

agreed.

"Better make another ceiling' pulley, Gypsy!" Tavy laughed.

Seeing Rahzvon's disapproval, Naomi quickly cut in, "Mother and Daniel send their regrets for not being here tonight. They went to get Pearl and the children for the celebration, tomorrow."

While Guillaume excitedly presented another crate, Allison sat somber at his side, envying it all— the marriage, the gifts, the party, everything of which she had dreamed. Trina, too, wished that she and Tavy were the guests of honor celebrating their engagement, but she was hopeful that it would not be in the too distant future.

Rahzvon helped Sophia open the umpteenth crate, housing a narrow cabinet from Livia. He offered the words that his dumbfounded wife could not speak, "Livia, it is magnificent! Thank you."

"You are quite welcome. My father purchased it in Italy, many years ago. I understand that it is circa sixteen hundred and sixty."

Sophia ran her fingers over the pulls, "Look, Rahzvon, there is a different scene painted on each panel—on the glass, too."

"So many drawers, Naomi commented, "a lovely conversation piece for your parl—"

"Yes, gorgeous," Rahzvon reiterated quietly, feeling embarrassed that their humble residence did not have a parlor to accommodate it, or any other room, for that matter.

Sophia left the rocking chair to hug Livia. "Positively, perfect!"

"I am glad that you like it." Livia smiled up at Hiram. He nodded.

Hannah offered two presents sitting on her lap. "These are from me, Sophia, Rahzvon."

"Mine is bigger," Sophia giggled. "Open yours first."

After removing the wrap, Rahzvon pulled the gold and enameled watch from the box. His eyes glistened while he read the inscription, "For My Son with Love." He could not breathe—his heart was bursting. He could not take his eyes from the extraordinary timepiece, or face the giver. All was quiet. He placed the watch ever so carefully in the velvet-lined box and pushed away the packing at his feet to make his way over to his mother-in-law. He offered Hannah a trembling hand to stand. The warmth of their embrace touched the hearts of everyone present. Rahzvon and Hannah exchanged no words, as they were not necessary. A minute later, they discreetly wiped their eyes and returned to their seats. Sophia touched Rahzvon cheek and offered her mother a grateful smile before opening her gift.

"Mother—how stately and elegant!"

"It is an *ecuelle*—to serve hot dishes. We spent so many years together in the café—I thought it to be appropriate."

Lifting the top, Sophia said, "Look, darling, the silver engraved lid is monogrammed with an 'S'. Our first official Sierzik piece."

Rahzvon rubbed Sophia's back and smiled appreciatively.

After reading Trina's card promising the new bride a shopping spree, Sophia opened Tavy's welcome quaich, the silver, double-handled cup. All the gifts were open, save one, and of course, Hiram's. The last gift, donning a white bunting bow, was compliments of the Zigmann family. The German, seventeenth century, oak and wrought iron strongbox immediately served the couple well. It provided room to store their many recently acquired valuables, until they would find space to display them. Leaving it at the manor was unquestionably the only safe place for it, until they procured a larger home.

Hiram then lifted Kade high above his head. "Well son, shall we tell them about our gift?"

The baby giggled as Hiram twirled him back and forth.

"Darling, be careful! He just had his milk!" Livia warned.

With that thought, Hiram quickly lowered Kade to his lap. And announced, "As we are about to become the proud owners of a fine vehicle, I believe that we can sacrifice one of our carriages, outfitted with two fine horses. Right, Kade?"

Sophia jumped up and embraced her uncle.

"That is a very generous gesture. We thank you for your gift and the celebration," Rahzvon said and shook Hiram's hand.

Naomi insisted that she and Edward host the gala event in the ballroom at Brachney Hall. Livia was grateful, as she had never planned a celebration of any kind. The pipers and drummers supplied the music and Eloise prepared tables of treats with the help of Naomi's staff and Sophia's taste-testing supervision.

The ballroom was filled to capacity with guests mingling in the corridor, as well. Nearly all invitations produced a guest—including Miss Nettlepin. She was not content to remain at home, unconvinced that Hiram would choose Miss Nichols over her. She arrived wearing most memorable attire, which she claimed to have designed and made herself. Unfortunately, the garish color combination was more befitting that of a circus clown, than that of the village schoolmarm.

As the festivities commenced, Kade enjoyed the loving arms of nearly every member of the family and village. The other children were entertained by the creativity of Guillaume and Allison. The former was often spotted hiding on the veranda within the heavy drapes, or peeking from behind a potted plant; the latter joined in on the fun, but as graciously as possible.

Rahzvon and Sophia's recent baby-attending adventures left them in want of some much-needed time alone together. They danced every dance and socialized very little—with exception to offering comments of gratitude for the gifts and the guests' attendance.

Hiram retreated safely to the company of the men after being wrangled into two dances with the determined Miss Nettlepin.

While Naomi flitted about, keeping a watchful eye on just about everything, Eloise kept the refreshment tables in good order. Maryanne Wheaton spent most of the evening chatting with her dearest friend, Harriet Dugan, while Beatrice, had the rare pleasure of enjoying the company of her daughter-in-law, Pearl.

The men were standing in an ever-growing group discussing motorcars from the seemingly endless line of Pierce Arrows, Columbia Baker Electric automobiles, Peerless, and the Argylls and Albions manufactured in Scotland. At one point, Joseph Dugan, head piper, became so involved in the conversation that he put down his pipes ending the music for nearly a quarter hour. His wife's reprimand and prodding hustled the musicians back to the platform to resume their duties.

The very sophisticated Trina Dunmore sat content with the handsome sailor in traditional Highland dress, Henry McTavish. She took a sip of her drink, "Do you remember the first time we met, Henry?"

"Aye—in this very room...or was it ou' in the hall where ye nearly slapped me?"

She grinned sheepishly, "It was all a miscommunication. How was I to know that you thought that I was soliciting your affections by means of Guillaume's ridiculous note?"

"No matter, a bit o' turbulence makes ye stronger for the next storm." Tavy patted her hand and smiled. He looked over her shoulder where Hiram was standing with Kade cradled in his arm. "Hiram will be good for the lad."

Trina turned to look. "Yes, he and Livia are good candidates for parenting."

"Aye...do ye think we are?"

"You and I?"

"Aye. Do ye think that we would be good parents?"

"Together?"

"O' course."

She sat down her goblet. "I had never considered it. It would be difficult—you going to sea for months at a time."

He leaned back and laughed, "It doesna take long to make a family."

"*Henry!* I was commenting on the fact that we, that is, if we were a family, we would be a broken family with me on land with the children—you on the boat."

"*Ship.* Nay, I wouldna be shippin' ou' and leave ye fendin' for yerself and the bairn, like me poor, dear mother. Nay, I would be findin' work in a shipyard."

"But, Tavy, you love the sea. You have spent most of your life on the water. I cannot believe that you would be content to give it up."

He picked up his fork and slid the tines across the empty plate for a few seconds before looking up at her.

"I wouldna give it up. There is an abandoned lighthouse that I hae been keepin' me eye on. Plenty o' room and could be verra bonnie wit' the help o' a willin' woman," he said cautiously.

"A lighthouse?" She smiled. "Sounds intriguing."

"Aye?" He sat up straighter. "I was thinkin' that we could buy a small dory and sail wit' the bairn on Sunday afternoons."

"Perhaps a sailboat...er, sailship."

Tavy laughed and smiled as though he had made the greatest catch of the season.

Daniel met Hiram at the refreshment table.

"Hiram, I've been thinkin' about the shop."

"Have you chosen a location? Will it be on the north side of the village or in the old Kraemer building next to the livery?"

"How did ya know? Hae ya spoken to Birdie?"

"Nay, but I know that nothing would make Beatrice happier than residing near Naomi. Am I right?" Hiram grinned.

"Aye," Daniel agreed.

Livia walked up from behind, carrying Kade. "Daniel, do not doubt it for a minute—Hiram is always right," she smiled and continued over to Maryanne and Harriet.

"Hiram, Kade may hae been orphaned, but I can safely say that he should be the envy o' ev'ry lad in Scotland, wit' ya two for parents."

"Thank you, my friend."

The following day, Hiram met with Livia in the west wing where Livia had chosen the rooms to utilize for her childcare facility. He entered the larger of the two rooms carrying a cup of tea.

"Good afternoon, Hiram."

"Good afternoon, Livy." His dimples appeared in hearing her usual greeting.

She spread her arms. "We shall begin here. I have decided to make this large room the common room where all the children will gather for group activities."

"Aye."

Livia led him to the far side of the room.

"This little room, over here, shall be for Kade and his friends—the infant nursery."

Hiram nodded and sipped his tea.

She stepped next to the adjacent room. "This other room shall be a storage room. Here is a special corner for individual learning and reading. Did you get a chance to see Daniel's wedding gift for Sophia and Rahzvon?"

"Aye, the eleventh edition of Encyclopaedia Britannica; a great addition to a future library." He clasped his hands together. "Well, it would seem that you have it all under control. Shall we go?"

"Go where? I am not finished discussing the arrangements," she said with disappointment.

"Continue then, but could we hasten it a bit? Gaelon's friends are arriving with their new motorcars. I want to be there when they arrive. I *am* the proprietor of this estate."

"You cannot fool me. That has nothing to do with it. You only want to see those vehicles at the very second that they arrive."

"Livy, how often do we get to see two new Argylls without leaving Lochmoor Glen?"

"How often do I ask for a few minutes of your time?"

"I promise that you may have my undivided attention for the rest of the evening—after they leave."

Livia sighed. "Very well."

Taking her hand, Hiram swept her down the hall. He was smiling like a boy going to his first pony show.

The motorcars did not arrive as scheduled, to Hiram's, Edward's, Daniel's, Gaelon's, Rahzvon's, Albert's, Guillaume's, Joseph Dugan's, and a few male servants' dismay. The women were curious to see the new models as well, but displayed little interest, being in solidarity with Livia, who could see her opportunity to discuss her hours of planning, flitting away with each passing minute.

Hours later, *the machine* arrived. The men left the mansion like bees stirred from their hive. The women discreetly peeked out the windows to admire the beautiful vehicles.

Time passed quickly while Gaelon's friends stayed for dinner and chatted late into the night.

Naomi, Beatrice, and Allison ordered a carriage and returned to Brachney Hall without Edward. The remaining women retired at ten, unnoticed, as the men were in deep discussion over the gas combustion engine. Sophia, the exception, fell asleep on the divan under Rahzvon's arm while Hannah walked upstairs with the very disappointed Livia, carrying Kade.

"Livia, you know how men are. It is like a new toy for them," Hannah consoled her.

"I know. Hiram was obligated to stay and talk."

"I am certain that tomorrow he will discuss the school with you."

"No, he cannot. He is going to help Daniel find a site for his new store. They expect to be gone most of the day, as there are several possible locations."

"Perhaps the day after tomorrow."

"No, he has a speech in Glasgow. Gaelon and Rahzvon are going with him. They shan't be back until very late that night."

"I am sorry, Livia, I have discovered that my brother does not always think before he speaks. I know you were anxious to discuss your plans with him, but I would be willing to listen, if you would like."

"I appreciate it, but I need to discuss the plans for the furnishings with him."

"Well, surely next week he can find time."

"Goodnight, Hannah."

Hannah leaned over and kissed her sleeping nephew's forehead. "Goodnight, Livia."

It was nearly two o'clock in the morning when Hiram entered the hall of the second floor. His head was still spinning with the excitement over his future motorcar purchase. Smiling broadly, he opened the door to his room.

"I cannot wait to tell Livy." He stopped dead in his tracks, realizing that time had slipped away. *Oh no, Livy.* He ran to her door, but the grandfather clock chimed but twice, alerting him to the hour. *It is too late.* He put his hands in his pockets, walked slowly back to his room, and closed the door. He pulled off his jacket and tossed it onto the bed and unbuttoned his shirt.

"I promised her," he lamented. He fell back on

the bed, rationalizing that he could apologize in the morning and discuss her school after breakfast. He sat up suddenly. "Blast it! I am leaving with Daniel." *Then there is the Glasgow meeting.* He hit his forehead with his palm. "Why do these things always happen to me?"

At the Sierzik cottage, Rahzvon left his slumbering wife in the carriage, hoisted the table, and pulled the bedrolls from the top shelf of the wardrobe. He spread them out and went to retrieve Sophia. He carried her into the cottage, laid her down on the floor, removed her shoes, and covered her. She never stirred. He took off his boots and lay down beside her thinking, *Uh...we need a mattress.* He looked over at Sophia who was turned with her back to him. He got up, went to her vanity and pulled out a ribbon from the drawer. He knelt down next to her and carefully braided her hair in a single braid and tied the ribbon to secure it.

He lay back down, staring at the table above them. He reached over to blow out the lantern when he glanced back up at the underside of the table. He squinted, stood up, hunched over, beneath it. There was an envelope, stained and yellowed with age. He removed it from the rusted nails that held it and moved closer to the lamp to examine it. He opened the envelope and silently read:

> To the reader of this:
> Know this—my imprisonment here and my
>   possible demise is the sole responsibility
> of Mr. McDonnally.   —Avera S

What? He read it again. He turned slowly to his sleeping wife and back to the incriminating note.

He put it back into the envelope. Sleep did not come easily for him.

At McDonnally Manor, Hiram, too, tossed and turned feeling miserable about the situation with Livia. He regretted the fact it was so very late, wishing he could awaken her and apologize. Unable to sleep, he put on his robe and went downstairs to get something to eat. The glow of light coming from the kitchen met him at the doorway. There, he was surprised to find the object of his insomnia sitting at the table with a glass of milk.

Livia looked up, but said nothing.

"Hello, Livy," he said with caution.

"Good morning, Hiram," she said with little interest.

Hiram poured a glass of milk for himself and sat down across from her. "Kade is sleeping...well?"

She raised a brow.

"Oh...would you like to discuss your plans now?" he asked cheerily.

Livia said nothing. Her disapproving glare was an answer in itself.

"Sorry, Livy. Time got away from me."

Livia looked around the room as though she did not hear him, finished her milk, and took the glass to the sink.

"Next week, I shall be available—except Monday, I have to prepare the report for the...the Tuesday meeting in Edinburgh. But Wednesday after the conference—I know that it will be late, but you could take an afternoon nap so that you could wait up for me."

Livia made direct eye contact, then shook her head, and left the kitchen. She continued down the hall.

Hiram called from the kitchen doorway, "I love you, Livy."

"I love you too, Hiram," she mumbled and went upstairs.

Rising later that morning was difficult for most of the members of the McDonnally household, due to their late night discussions. Hiram arrived at the breakfast table famished, but exhausted. Livia was less chipper than usual and Gaelon and Daniel were more reserved. Gaelon's friends also joined the McDonnally group in the dining room, as they had spent the night at the mansion as Hiram's guests. It was not long before the discussion was consumed by talk of the motorcars. Hiram became so involved in the conversation that Kade's cries went unnoticed.

Livia went to calm the baby, feeling somewhat resentful in that she had spent most of the earlier hours attending to the restless infant, while Hiram slept. She and Kade retired to the peace of the parlor without Hiram's objection or acknowledgement. Livia found some consolation in the fact, that in all fairness, Hiram needed his rest in order to be attentive during his excursion with Daniel, while she would be free to nap later that day with Kade.

After Gaelon's friends left the estate, Hiram remained in the portal to get one last gander of the elaborate departing motorcars. He sighed with satisfaction and went to see Livia before leaving with Daniel.

"Well, Love, you have a pleasant day with our son and I promise to take more time for the two of you, very soon." He went over to the cradle, "Take care of your mother, lad." He stood before Livia who was quiet and downcast. Hiram lifted her chin.

"Livy, I do apologize." He took her in his arms

and attempted to make up for his negligence.

For Livia, the kiss was adequate consolation for his transgressions. She picked up Kade. Hiram kissed his forehead.

"See you soon, Livy."

Livia guided Kade's little hand in a waving motion as Hiram passed through the archway.

A few hours later, Eloise's gentle voice wakened Livia from her nap on the divan.

"Miss Nichols, there is someone here to speak with you."

Livia opened her eyes to see Eloise's troubled expression and a young, uniformed soldier standing in the hall.

"You may go in, sir," Eloise announced and fled to the kitchen.

He entered the room as Livia rose.

"Good afternoon, Miss." He bowed at the waist. "My name is Lt. Mark Brenin. I had hoped to speak with Mr. McDonnally, as well, but I understand that he is out for the day."

Brenin? "Yes...yes he is. Excuse me, I am Livia—Livia Nichols."

"Aye. I have been informed of the fact that you and Mr. McDonnally have taken charge of my cousin's son."

She could barely speak the words, "Your cousin's son?"

"Aye—the child of the woman who lost her life in the accident, Mum. I have the official papers."

Livia's eyes widened fearfully. "Papers? For what?"

Chapter VI

"The Gift"

"Where did you come from, baby dear?
Out of everywhere into here.

But how did you come to us, you dear?
God thought about you, and so I am here."

—George MacDonald

"Papers?" Livia whispered.

"I have come to take the lad to live with my wife and me," the lieutenant explained gently, seeing her distressed response.

"That cannot be; we were told that there was no kin to be found."

He handed her the paper. "Aye, I was on duty in Africa. We only recently received notification of the accident from my cousin's friend."

Livia looked to the quiet cradle and then clutched the arm of the divan. He helped to steady her to sit. She began reading through the papers.

"Mum, I can see that this comes as a frightful shock to you. You need to understand that our wives, my cousin's and mine, were the best of friends. We are the infant's godparents. For us it is a bittersweet blessing; we have lost our dear cousin, but now have a son. Yes, my wife will no longer spend her days alone."

Livia sat stunned. The lieutenant walked over to the cradle. He looked down on the sleeping infant for the first time.

His voice cracked, "The spittin'" image of his father." He carefully picked up Kade and cuddled him close to his chest. The baby did not waken. "He looks perfect—healthy and well-cared for. Please extend my gratitude to Mr. McDonnally, as well." He stared in wonder at the infant. "You know, I was not present at the christening."

Christening?

He lifted Kade to his shoulder. "The documents are yours to keep. I am sorry, Miss Nichols. I realize this is a tremendous disappointment. If you would like to set up an occasional visit with Thomas, our address is noted in the document."

Thomas? Livia noted the irony in that Kade bore the name of Livia's past suitor—a man Hiram loathed. Seeing the lieutenant starting toward the archway, she panicked, "But, sir, I cannot release him without Mr. McDonnally's permission."

"Miss Nichols, I am tardy as it is."

Livia chased after him into the hall.

"The papers are in order, Mum, and I have to leave immediately. My wife is to arrive in London today. She is waiting for us."

"But Hiram—"

"I am very sorry."

"His things!"

"I have a nursemaid waiting in the carriage and we brought everything we shall need. My wife and I thank you."

Clutching the curtain framing the sidelight, Livia sobbed watching the carriage move forward. It was taking her baby boy away. She felt her heart being ripped from her chest; a voice screamed in her head, pleading for the carriage to stop and return. Trembling, she squinted through the burning tears that slipped down her face. The back of the vanishing vehicle was now a tiny black box in the distance. A second later, the drive was empty. She blinked several times in an attempt to clear her vision, but it was true. It was real. Kade was gone.

"No!" she screamed.

Rahzvon's arms tightened around her—holding her together. Rahzvon, the ideal comforter, spoke to her softly, "I know...I know." He was all too familiar with loss—the helplessness, the inability to stop the inevitable. He had been forced to watch his father's execution and Kade was his baby, too.

The next few hours, Livia lay on her bed next to the empty cradle. She tossed and turned anxiously trying to make sense of this nightmare that destroyed the promising future with Hiram and Kade. It had obliterated their little family's life together and she needed to know why.

My poor baby, what will you think when you waken to strangers? Will you be frightened?

The truth whispered in her head, *Kade is with family. They love him.*

"But we love him!"

The soldier's words returned, "We are the infant's godparents. The spittin' image of his father." *He was christened Thomas.*

Livia rolled to her back, when she realized. *He is not our Kade anymore. He is their Thomas.* She glared up at the canopy's blue lace ruffle, reminding her of Kade's gown. Their christening was never to be. He was already Thomas Brenin, never to become Kade McDonnally.

She looked over at the cradle. She remembered it all: the parenting, the sleepless nights, the pacing, the singing, and Kade's smiles. Hiram's smiles. There had been no time for goodbyes and besides, Kade was asleep. It was for the best; she knew that she could not have said good-bye, nor could Hiram, as it would have been unbearable. She wiped her eyes and glanced at the rocking chair next to the bed.

Why did you come to us, sweet, sweet, baby? She closed her eyes for a minute and then opened them. *Because we had to share that love for you— brief as it was.* Now, she wondered how she would ever convince Hiram of that. She stared up at the canopy, remembering the day of their first outing as a family. *You loved me, Kade, and I will always love and remember you.*

***

Hiram arrived at his home later that evening. He was carrying two packages tucked under his arm and wearing a broad smile. He walked immediately to the parlor, which he found to be vacant.

"Livy!" he shouted up the staircase.

Eloise appeared in the hall from the kitchen. Her solemn face alerted Hiram to ominous news.

Eloise wiped hers eyes with her apron. "Miss Nichols is in your study, sir." She darted back to the kitchen.

With long strides and a feeling of concern and confusion, Hiram went to find Livia. He opened the doors to see her sitting in a chair by the window. He entered the room and closed the doors behind him.

"Livy?"

She looked up with troubled eyes. She had been crying.

"Sit down, Hiram."

Hiram pulled up a chair and anxiously sat down next to her and placed the packages on the side table.

"Please, tell me. What is it, Livy?"

"We had a visitor this afternoon."

"Who?" he asked nervously.

"A soldier. Lieutenant Mark Brenin."

Hiram froze. The implications were apparent by Livia's grief stricken expression. He immediately asked the dreaded question.

"Where is Kade?"

Livia swallowed hard. "He has gone to live with his kin—the man and his wife are Kade's godparents. The lieutenant is the cousin of Kade's father."

An excruciating pain shot through Hiram's chest. His eyes darted wildly around the room as he pulled himself from the chair. He could not move. It could not be possible.

He swung around, horrified and shouted, *"How could you let him take him?"*

Livia drew back fearfully. He started to pace, but had no sense of direction. Livia held her breath. "Was there any proof of this man's identity?" he bellowed.

Trembling, she lifted her hand and pointed toward the desk, "Yes—the documents."

Hiram snatched the papers, quickly scanned them, tore them to shreds, and threw them to the side. He retreated to the far side of the room in silence. Livia watched, feeling his pain and left her chair to console him, but he stormed out—slamming the doors into the pockets. From the window, she saw him moving slowly down the road toward Brachney Hall. *My poor, sweet man.* She lowered her head and closed her eyes. She then opened them focused on the packages on the table. She picked up the small one, knowing it must be Hiram's gift for the son, who was no longer theirs. Her nervous fingers reverently returned it to the table. *Oh, Hiram.* She then ran from the house and caught up with Hiram, entering the woods dividing the two estates.

"Hiram!"

He stopped, but did not face her. She moved next to him and took his hand. He stood for a minute, and then looked down at her, his dark eyes staring intensely upon her. He slid his hand from her grasp, but she lifted his arm and moved beneath it. Together they entered the path through the woods.

The next few days were difficult as Hiram and Livia could not spend them together. Hurt and angry, Hiram continued with his busy schedule, avoiding time for the necessary grieving. Life was very melancholy at the Sierzik cottage, as well. Coping with the loss of their little *cayden* did not come easily to either. Rahzvon was now comforting Sophia on several occasions.

When Hiram returned from his final obligation for the coming fortnight, he sat on the divan with his arm around Livia. Neither party had mentioned Kade and would not for some time.

"How are the plans coming for your school?" he asked.

"I have changed my mind a dozen times. I guess the extra time I was given, was for the best. I believe that I would have regretted some of my original decisions."

"Tomorrow, bright and early, we shall discuss any renovations and provisions you desire." He kissed her forehead.

"I hope that I can make a decision by then."

"Not to worry, I shall help. If there is one area of which I am qualified, it is decision making. And now, my beautiful lass, you need to get some sleep, it is nearly midnight."

"Hiram?"

"Aye?"

"Could we take a holiday to Zurich—go to those places that we frequented when we first met?"

"We shall leave the day after tomorrow."

Livia snuggled next to him. "Hiram?"

"Aye?"

"Could we stay here tonight, together?" she whispered.

He ran his fingers through her hair and looked to the spot where the cradle once sat. "I was hoping you would ask."

Hiram blew out the lamp. They spent the night in each other arms on the divan. Life had brought another change for Hiram, a necessary one, and in his best interest.

Despite their grieving for Kade, Rahzvon and Sophia prepared for their postponed trip to Brussels. Rahzvon secured a caretaker for their tiny cottage, housing the very expensive piece of furniture. Sophia fussed with her limited wardrobe, unsure as to what to take for the trip.

Rahzvon's knowledge of the contents of the mysterious envelope, which he found attached beneath the table, was aggravating, but he made the difficult decision that it would remain a secret from Sophia until they had left Scotland. He could not risk her approaching the clan with many questions until he had the opportunity for further investigation.

Hiram put on his jacket preparing to leave for Zurich. He made a final check around the room when he saw the little package sitting on the table by the door to his bedchamber. He stared at it fearfully as one does a wasp invading one's home, knowing that going too close would only put him in risk for more pain. It was his first gift for Kade. He had imagined the baby's delight in receiving it—the giggles and coos. Now it lay idle, bringing pain, rather than joy. His first thought was to dispose of it, but tossing away the memory of the son who had first made the three of them a family, seemed a near sacrilege.

He closed the door and paused next to the package. *Nay*, he thought. It did not seem right to save it, or to present it to their first child. He continued downstairs where he met Eloise and Livia in the hall.

Having difficulty speaking, Hiram instructed, "Eloise, please deliver the package on the table outside my bedchamber...to the Wheaton infant."

"Yes, sir."

Livia felt the pain return. Kade was truly gone forever.

While the baggage was loaded into the carriage, Rahzvon and Sophia arrived.

"Wait!" Sophia called out, "We have passage with you!"

Hiram lowered his head, shook it, and laughed. He looked questionably to Livia, being skeptical of travelling with his unpredictable niece and her outspoken husband. She smiled.

"Very well, make haste. Transfer the Sierzik bags to our carriage!" He motioned to the servants when Gaelon rode up in a state of alarm.

"I received a wire from my colleagues! The Archduke of Austria and his wife, Sophia, were assassinated!"

Sophia instantly cringed at the thought of the fate of the woman sharing her name.

"What does this mean?" Rahzvon asked Hiram whose face was grave with concern.

"I am not certain, but I think we should postpone our holiday for the time being," Hiram said woefully and looked apologetically toward Livia. "I am sorry, Love. I have a great deal invested in those two countries. I can only imagine where this may lead."

It was soon very apparent that the assassination was, indeed, the beginning of a major change and political unrest. Hiram stood in the hall with a handful of envelopes from the morning mail delivery. He shook his head with despair for his state of affairs, as the conflict had turned the world upside down. His business connections in Austria and Germany were in need of re-evaluation.

Sophia approached him from behind, carrying a plate of teacakes. "Good morning, Uncle Hiram."

"Good morning, Sophia." He turned and looked to the plate. "Morning treats, for the ladies?"

"No, no one is hungry, except me. I cannot imagine why. It has been nearly an hour since breakfast." She entered the parlor where Naomi and Livia were chatting.

Hiram wrinkled his brow at her comment and entered his study.

Sophia carried her plate of goodies to the rocking chair and sat down. "What is the topic of conversation, today—need I ask." She spread her napkin across her lap.

"If this conflict escalates to a war, it will bring many changes," Naomi said solemnly.

"Agnes Murray told me that Jake is joining the army if Britain becomes involved," Sophia mentioned before indulging in her first teacake.

"Are they still to be wed?" Naomi asked.

"The wedding is postponed. Agnes is beside herself. Jake says he shan't have her widowed before she is twenty-three."

"Hopefully it will be resolved before long. Poor dear. Such a worry and his parents went to such trouble to fix up the cottage for them." Naomi sighed and sat back.

"Well, I am glad I am Mrs. Sierzik. I would have just died if Rahzvon went off to fight without marrying me." She took another bite when she saw her husband standing in the archway. She turned quickly to return the plate to the side table when the tearing of the seam of her blouse broke the silence. "Oh, no." Sophia twisted to survey the damage.

Rahzvon shook his head. "If you would ease up on the teacakes, this would cease from happening. It is the third blouse this week," he scorned.

Sophia's eyes widened, "How dare you! Do I complain every time that you take a second helping?" she retaliated.

"I am not the one in need of a new wardrobe every week."

Sophia's jaw dropped, just before the flood of tears. She shot past him and up the stairs.

"Phia!" he called after her in frustration. He looked to Naomi and Livia who immediately turned away, keeping any comment to themselves. He then turned toward the study to Hiram's solicitation.

"Come on in, Mr. Sierzik."

Rahzvon sat in his brooding state and scowled. "What am I to do with your belligerent niece?"

"Easy man, you are talking about the woman you love most in the world."

"Mr. McDonnally, she is becoming intolerable. She used to be a pleasure, adventuresome, full of life. Now all she does is eat and sleep."

"Sounds like one who is bored."

"Bored? I asked to take her for a ride up to Duncan Ridge, yesterday. Do you know what her reply was?"

"Nay."

"She said she did not want to leave because Eloise's berry cobbler would be coming out of the oven in twenty minutes."

Hiram left his chair. "She has to get her mind on something other than food. She would have, had she not married and instead gone to school, as I had wanted," Hiram stated looking down at the slumping husband.

Rahzvon looked away. "We shan't go into that. Besides she would have not been enrolled, as yet."

"Speaking of schools, Livy can always use some assistance."

"I hope so. Keeping Phia at home is not an option. She says it makes her claustrophobic. She is the one who wanted that monstrosity dressing table that fills the entire room."

Hiram walked to the window, "I beg to differ with you, but her furniture choice would not have appeared quite so monstrous had the home been larger. Your financial state could afford a larger home than that tiny, one-room bread box."

"Yes, it could, but your niece cannot maintain order in even that one room."

"Sophia has had the benefits of maids and servants for some time now. I can understand her reluctance to perform domestic chores; she worked during her childhood."

"Mr. McDonnally, you cannot let men live like pigs!"

"Hmm? *Very* good—I am impressed—you quoting Jacob Riis."

"Seriously, last night I washed the dishes, hung up the table, and washed out her stockings because she was too tired from her visit with Agnes Murray. All they did was *converse*."

Hiram laid his hand on Rahzvon's shoulder. "Son, you and Sophia have a lot of years ahead of you. I suggest that you lay down the ground rules, now."

Rahzvon got up, "I will try, but I guarantee, it will not go well. I merely suggested that she cut down on teacakes and she ran off crying."

"It is important that you be charming, and irresistible in your technique, but stern. A woman wants her man to take charge."

He asked suspiciously, "Does Livia agree with that philosophy?"

Hiram looked away. "Of course...of course, she does," he said weakly.

Dubious, Rahzvon nodded. He revisited the contents of the mysterious letter. He had heard enough advice from one whose character may be in question and headed for the door. "I have to take her to the jeweler's now. We need to see what can be done about the wedding band I ordered; it is suddenly too small."

In the parlor, Livia and Naomi respectfully refrained from any discussion of the Sierziks' marital problems.

"What will Edward do if Britain becomes involved?" Livia asked Naomi.

"I am certain that he will do all that he can from the home-front. He is nearly forty-two and not exactly fit for duty, since his fall from the ladder."

"Hiram, too. I hope that the farm families will accept his help without resentment for his pacifism."

"Farm families? He is offering them financial assistance? Not that I would expect anything less of him."

"Actually, after the village meeting, he met with several of the families, including his tenants. They refused any charity, although many of the husbands and sons could be going off to serve. So, Hiram insisted that he and the staff would assist with the chores."

"Hiram doing farm work? Other than working with the horses, I was unaware of his experience in agrarian duties."

"He has very little, but when Hiram wants to learn something, he jumps in and attacks it with an obsession. He proved that at the clock shop in Switzerland." Livia folded her hands in her lap. "The difficulty will arise when he is obligated to work under the instruction of the farm women."

"Absolutely. I have not known him to be fond of taking orders from whom he considers to be the weaker sex."

"Hiram really has no other option."

"I have no other option? In what regard?" he interrupted, entering the room.

"No other option, but to take me for a ride to the mercantile to pick up my order for my school." She jumped from her seat. "I need to make haste. I hope to have the grand opening very soon."

"Very well, I am at your service—a man of engaging conversation and a strong back for carrying your packages."

His use of the word 'engaging' tugged at Livia's heartstrings. *I wonder if he will ever propose.*

"Come along, Livy, fetch your bonnet."

Naomi walked them to the hall and bid them good day.

"Good day, Naomi, we will talk again, soon," Livia said, taking Hiram's arm.

Rahzvon entered Sophia's old room and found her sitting at the vanity, powdering her nose.

"Phia, I want to speak with you."

She ignored him.

"Could you please turn around and listen to

what I have to say?" he asked gently.

Sophia dropped the puff from a good foot above the vanity table and turned around very slowly with a look of indifference.

"That is better," he said, taking a seat on the bed a few feet from her. "We are both a little distracted with the news of the world events and with Kade—well...I think that you need something to entertain you—a *teemspit*. What would you call it?"

"A team spit?" That sounds disgusting!"

"You know, a hobby, like knitting."

"Knitting? *Really*, Rahzvon. I have plenty to do and very little time to do it."

"What might that be, Phia?"

"I have to return to clean, wash the dishes, visit with my family and friends."

Hearing her response, Rahzvon scanned the room trying to control his temper, but failed. "You do *not* clean or wash the dishes—I do. All you do is..." He tightened his fists and left the room leaving Sophia sitting motionless without expression. Her most acclaimed "better" half brooded in the hall, leaning against the wall with his arms folded across his chest. Hiram paused at the top of the stairs, and gestured for him to get back in there and fight for his rights. The perturbed husband scowled, lowered his head and with a hopeless nod, returned to the battlefield.

He entered the room, finding Sophia sitting cross-legged on the bed, fiddling with her old, rag doll, Charity.

"You do not want a wife," she spoke without looking at him, "you want a maidservant."

"I could certainly use one, our home looks more often like a pigsty, than not."

"It is no bigger than one," Sophia said smugly.

Rahzvon stepped over to the foot of the bed. "Phia, what has happened to you? I can remember a time when you offered to cook and wash my clothing, so that you could come to Kosdrev with me."

"That was before we were married," she stated matter-of-factly. She lay back on the pillow.

Rahzvon walked over to the door. "I cannot continue to live like this. It would never be acceptable in Kosdrev. This is all going to stop. We are going home. We will continue this conversation there. Phia? Phia?"

The conversation would have to wait. Sophia was sound asleep, snoring comfortably.

Rahzvon let out a sigh and sat down next to her. "Little One, whatever am I going to do with you?"

Sophia did not stir. He pulled the cover up over her, kissed her cheek, and quietly left the room. He took refuge on the front steps of Hiram's home where he found the pleasure of Marvel Wheaton's company.

"Hullo, Master Sierzik."

"Good morning, Marvel."

"Look what I hae."

Rahzvon lifted the volume from her little hands and read the cover. *The American Girls Handy Book.* "What is this—preliminary instruction in how to perform the tasks of a wife and mother? Phia, could use one," he mumbled, leafing through the pages.

"Eh? It is an instuctin' book. Mr. O'Leardon special ordered it for Master Edward. He gave it to me and me sisters—he brought it yesterday. It is me turn to study it. Ye can make dolls out o' cornhusks, a paper daisy fan, and even a telephone from boxes and string. I am goin' to ask Mrs. Zigmann for empty boxes. We hae only tins."

"Please, don't show this to my wife." He handed it back to Marvel.

"Why, sir?"

"Uh...she has plenty to do, already." He rubbed his forehead.

"Sir, ye look a wee bit troubled."

"Marvel, it is difficult being a grown-up, at times."

"Ye need not worry, I should think that ye would be a grand father." She giggled, "A *grand* father... not a grandfather."

"That really is not a concern, as yet, Marvel."

"Aye, but spring will verra soon come, before ye can say, Sophia's Secret!" Marvel smiled and sat down next to him.

He looked at her curiously. "Sophia's secret?"

"Aye, Mrs. Dugan told Mama that Sophia is always tired and hungry. But Dunna worry, 'bout it. It shall pass in a fortnight or two. Mama always felt better, later on." She opened the book. "I canna wait to see yer bairn. It will be beautiful, I am quite sure."

Rahzvon's eyes widened and stared blankly at her. He swallowed hard and stood up. *Bairn?* "Excuse me, Marvel...I have an errand."

"Good day, Master Sierzik."

In his dazed state, Rahzvon turned and stepped from the porch and through the door. He entered the staircase.

The voracious appetite, the desire to sleep all the time, the shrinking clothes, the ill-fitting wedding band? The wedding band—it has been but a few weeks since I presented it to her. He remembered that her face was glowing. *Glowing!*

It all seemed to make sense. He hesitated on the steps. He was going to be a father.

From the study, Hiram watched the bewildered

young man and left his desk. "Rahzvon? What is it, now?"

Rahzvon, pale and speechless, faced him.

"Lad, come sit down. You look poorly." Hiram led him into the parlor. "Did you not resolve your issues with Sophia?"

Rahzvon slowly shook his head, nodded, and then shrugged, looking baffled.

"Speak to me, man," Hiram demanded.

"I...I never thought...I know, but..."

Hiram knitted his brows. "Son, you are not making sense."

Sophia spoke from the hall, "Rahzvon, I am ready to go home to wash the dishes and do the laundry."

Hiram cracked a smile and patted Rahzvon's back. "You see, son? All is well." Hiram leaned over and said discreetly, "Good job."

Rahzvon gave Hiram an immediate double take for the irony of his compliment and then moved slowly toward Sophia. He picked her up, as though she were a delicate, porcelain teacup.

"Rahzvon?" she said with surprise.

Focused on Sophia's puzzled countenance, he announced, "I love you, Phia," and then made his way to the door.

Hiram followed and gladly opened it for them. "Remember. Dinner. Eloise's fried fish." He remained in the portal stroking his beard. "Hmm? Charming, but stern. Aye, good job, lad."

"Rahzvon?" Sophia squeezed his arm.

"*Phia*," was the only word he spoke while lifting her into the carriage. He climbed up beside her and drove slowly home, watching for potholes and bumps in the road.

Chapter VII

"Grand Father"

"Ye faithful saints, fresh courage take,
The clouds ye so much dread
Are big with mercy and shall break
In blessings on your head."

—William Cowper

Sophia sat fearfully, wondering what thoughts motivated Rahzvon's amorous behavior. She had never seen him behave in this manner.

When they arrived at their tiny residence, Rahzvon jumped from the seat and tied the horses. Instead of offering the usual hand to Sophia, he lifted her down, carried her into the cottage, and sat her on one of the two chairs. He took the one across from her. Sophia observed him with curious wonder.

"Phia, I do not want to upset you, but you should know that I—"

"Rahzvon, please tell me," she said, nervously scrunching the fabric of her skirt.

He blurted it out, "I am going to be a father!"

Her immediate objection became all too clear when her right palm met his cheek with surprising speed and force. She flew from her chair screeching, "You unfaithful beggarpig!"

Rahzvon's face filled with horror at her misconception. He quickly grabbed her by the shoulders.

"Never touch me again!" she cried, pulling his hands from her.

"No, Phia! Not me—we...*We* are going to be a father!"

"What?" she demanded. Her face was now contorted with anger and confusion.

"I know—I know about our baby!" he pleaded.

Then there was silence.

Sophia glared at him through a blur of tears. *"Our* baby?"

"Please, sit down, you need to be calm. I never intended to upset you. Please forgive me," he said helping her to her chair.

Flabbergasted, she asked, "Why would you *say* such a thing?"

"It is all right, Phia. Marvel—Marvel Wheaton told me."

"Marvel Wheaton!" She stared, perplexed.

He hesitated, "Yes, my love, you no longer have to keep your secret from me."

"My secret?" She looked into his innocent, caring eyes and fell back into the chair.

"The symptoms were all apparent. Foolish man that I am, I just never recognized them. I feel terrible about reprimanding you for your need to eat and sleep." He brought the hand that had slapped his still reddened cheek to his lips and kissed it.

Symptoms? She considered the possibility for the first time. She lowered her gaze to her ever-growing belly. Tears instantly fell to her lap.

"Phia, it is alright. The surprise is not spoiled. I am ecstatic—a bit in shock, but thrilled—even if it was sooner than we planned."

"Rahzvon, you do not understand. I am as surprised as you are." She stared fearfully at her stomach. "I should have known." She then began to cry.

"You didn't know? Oh, my poor, sweet Little One." He hugged her. "Well, my love, at least we were surprised together."

Sophia could not stop crying.

"I hope these are tears of joy." He wiped the tears from her cheek with his finger. "You did want a baby sooner than eighteen months," he said tenderly pulling a curl away from her reddened eyes.

She nodded pathetically. "But...but I am afraid."

Rahzvon instinctively picked her up and looked around the room for another place to sit with her. No couch, no bed, only the second chair. He sat with her across his lap, her arms tight around him.

He could feel her warm tears trickling down his bare neck. Before he had a chance to offer more comforting words of support, the chair beneath them began to creak. A second later, they fell backwards and hit the floor.

Sandwiched between the broken chair and Sophia, Rahzvon asked in near panic, "Are you hurt?"

"Never better," she giggled and climbed off him. "Our baby and I thank you for cushioning the fall." She laughed, helping him to his feet.

"Are you sure that the baby is fine?"

"We are both fine."

He smiled, "Little Mama, you may love this cottage, but we are moving to a real house, immediately." He pulled her close. "Besides, I am not fond of the idea of our baby's cradle hanging from the ceiling."

Sophia hugged his waist. "I love you—wonderful father of my baby."

He said placing a hand across her belly, "I love you, too, my Little Ones."

"You do forgive me for slapping you? I am sorry that I called you a beggarpig. You do know that I believe that you would never be unfaithful?"

"You had better know that," he said, grinning.

"Rahzvon?"

"Yes?"

"Please, tell me—when are you informing Uncle Hiram of our baby?"

"Never. You are."

Disturbed by financial worries by day and haunted by nightmares of Kade's absence, Hiram was already suffering. He wearily made his way downstairs to meet with Livia.

Upon entering the parlor, his voice thundered throughout the first floor. "Nay! Eloise!"

Eloise arrived immediately. "Good morning, sir."

"Good, it is not! What goes on here? Please, tell me who is responsible for this disaster? Who moved everything?" He scanned the room where nothing was in its original position. The divan was in front of the window seat, the rocking chair next to the window, and the other chairs and tables were scattered about.

"Sir...Albert and—"

"Albert? You tell your husband to confine his creative endeavors to the cottage and return my furniture to its original position, at once!"

"Yes, sir, but—"

"Now, Mrs. Zigmann! Excuse me. I am going to my study where I hope to find some peace of mind. Please tell Miss Nichols to meet there with me."

Eloise watched Hiram cross the hall to the study. He glanced back at her fixed position, noting that her nervous finger had sought refuge to her mouth.

"Make haste!" He gestured and entered the pocket doors. "AGH! Eloise!" He swung around to meet her sour expression. "Has the man gone mad? Was the parlor not enough? He obviously has too much leisure time on his hands. Well, that will end when we begin our rounds on the farms. After he finishes with the parlor, notify him to get in here and clean up this mess! Look at this—my desk, my chairs, everything is helter-skelter!"

"But, sir—"

"Now, Eloise. It looks as though a twister passed through here," he said dragging his chair back several feet from the misplaced desk.

"Yes, sir." She shook her head with despair and

turned to carry out his orders when she found Livia standing before her. "Mum, I think—"

"Was he surprised? Was he pleased? Never mind." Livia confidently entered the room.

"But, Mum—"

Thrilled with the prospect of receiving Hiram's approval, Livia approached him. He stood with his arms folded across his chest scrutinizing the arrangement.

"Good morning, Hiram."

He turned toward her. "Good morning, Love. Did you ever witness such a horrific disaster?"

"Disaster?" she replied blankly.

"Aye—furniture here and there—no semblance of organization, whatsoever. Albert must be going through some sort of creative phase."

"Albert?"

"Aye, but he shall soon undo this calamity."

"Oh? I think that having the desk next to the window is actually quite ingenious, if you think about it. There you would have an excellent view overlooking the moors...while you are working."

"I need no view while I am working and I do not need the grounds men gawking at me while I am doing so."

Feeling disappointed, Livia made another attempt and hurried over to the chairs placed in the corner. "This is nice with the two chairs and the small table between them—a conversation nook of sorts," she suggested, smiling.

"Nay, they belong next to the hearth. Livy, I cannot believe that you would agree with Albert and this insanity."

That comment was more than she could bear. She fled from the room. Her plan to give the rooms a new look to help them move on, after Kade, had failed.

"Livy!" He chased after her. He met Eloise and Albert in the hall where he verbally attacked Albert, "This is entirely your fault, Zigmann. If you would have left things in their rightful place, Livy would not have agreed with you."

"Now, see here!" Albert protested.

Eloise latched onto her husband's arm to calm him, but he continued with his defense.

"Mr. McDonnally, I was hired to follow orders and that is what I did. I acted entirely on Miss Nichol's instruction. In fact, I warned her and tried to reason with her. I suggested that she confer with you first, but she would not listen. She wanted it to be a surprise."

"A surprise?" Hiram asked anxiously. "Eloise, why did you not tell me?"

"I tried, but—"

He stared blankly at the staircase.

"Sir, should we—" Eloise began.

"Leave it as it is," Hiram mumbled, ascending the stairs.

He slowed his pace as he approached the door to Livia's room. He paused and then knocked. Livia did not respond. He knocked again. Nothing. He cracked the door open and looked inside. He immediately panicked in seeing her sitting upon the railing of the balcony, high above the garden. He approached her slowly, afraid to speak. He swallowed hard and stepped onto the veranda. Through trembling lips, he spoke, "Livy...Livy, I am sorry."

Livia turned. Her flushed cheeks were tear-stained. "It is all right, Hiram, you shall never have to worry about me interfering with your affairs...ever again." She turned back toward the garden.

Hiram's fear immediately escalated to terror. He could not breathe. He struggled to plea, "Nay, Livy, I love you...I have had second thoughts! I have become accustom to the new furniture arrangements...I am de...delighted," he stammered.

"You need not humor me," she replied without turning.

"Livy, darling, let us go inside. Let me apologize—a kiss, to show my appreciation," he offered fearfully.

"Please, leave me alone. I will leave you to make the arrangements." She repositioned herself.

Hiram gasped, "Nay, Livy! I beg you! I shan't make the arrangements!"

Then, she turned and slipped down to the veranda floor. She reached up and touched his cheek. "Hiram, calm down. All right, rest assured that from now on I will take charge of all the decorating. You do not have to worry about it for a moment longer." She took his hand and walked him, in his dazed state, to a chair. He sat down.

She consoled him, "I know that your business affairs have been very distressing—the house is but a trivial matter for you. I have dozens of ideas to refurbish it. You shan't recognize it, once I am finished." She smiled encouragingly.

Perplexed, stressed, and tired, Hiram fought to ascertain how this situation evolved.

Livia continued, "I can see that you are exhausted. Come sit with me on the rail." She tugged on his hand.

He resisted, feeling that this inexplicable nightmare had crept into his waking hours.

"Come along, Hiram. It is quite invigorating. Do you remember the evening when we sat on the roof of the clock shop? I just love heights."

Hiram stood firm. His brows slowly came together. She had never considered jumping and he had never considered relinquishing his control of the redecorating of his home—but he had.

The European conflict brought Edward's mutual concern for the McDonnally holdings, as well as, one of Edward's dearest friends, Desilama Raheleka. Naomi and Edward were preparing a list of duties to winterize their home on the evening that the servant announced Mr. Raheleka's arrival. Edward immediately left his chair to greet his comrade of many years.

"My dear friend, welcome." Edward embraced the tall, mid-eastern gentleman.

"Edward." Desilama hugged him in return.

"You are always full of surprises, but I wager that I know what has brought you here," Edward said ominously.

Desilama gave him a distraught nod of confirmation.

"Hello, Desilama," Naomi greeted.

He reached for her hand and kissed it. "So, he finally came to his senses. Your second wedding ceremony was something I had always hoped to witness. I apologize for my absence at the blessed event."

Naomi smiled, "We missed you, but we understood. Thank you, again, for the lovely gift. The coverlet looks divine on our bed."

Edward smiled, then frowned. "Aye, we needed one. Heidi destroyed the quilt that I had given Naomi."

Naomi grinned sympathetically at Edward and changed the sensitive subject. "Desilama, how is your sister, since the train accident?"

"Thank you for asking. She is finally mobile—on the mend and walking, now. She has worked very hard and has made considerable progress."

"That is grand," Edward offered, escorting the guest to the drawing room. "Once she is up to it, you must bring her for a visit."

"She would be delighted with the invitation. We thank you."

"And you, my fine man, are we to receive an invitation to your wedding?" Edward asked directing Desilama to the sofa.

"Unfortunately, that is not possible. My former fiancé left the country with my *former* assistant."

"Sorry, old man. It must be an epidemic—my nephew's fiancé abandoned him, as well."

"*Edward,*" Naomi reprimanded in a whisper.

"Hiram, eh?" Desilama questioned.

"Aye, but, he did not suffer for long. He found a pretty, little—" Edward began.

"Edward!" Naomi cut him off. "Desilama, Livia Nichols is a bright, intelligent woman, who has known Hiram for years."

"Livia Nichols, the American playwright?"

Edward rolled his eyes with dread. "You saw the play?"

"Please, tell me that the character, 'Hiram,' was not portraying *your nephew.*"

Edward nodded.

"Desilama, do yourself a favor, and never mention it to Hiram *or* Livia, for that matter," Naomi warned.

He grinned. "I understand."

Edward left his chair. "Shall we go to the library? We have a lot to discuss. I welcome your advice and consultation. I am concerned about the Garnett contract," Edward said seriously.

"Yes, a major transaction."

"Please excuse me, I promised to speak with Allison," Naomi said, leaving.

"Give Allison my regards and tell her that I will meet with her later," Desilama replied.

"I will and I shall see you in the morning. Goodnight, dearest," Naomi gave a little wave.

"Goodnight, love!" Edward called out.

"Wonderful woman, Naomi," Desilama remarked.

"None better," Edward agreed.

Naomi tapped on her daughter's bedroom door. "Come in."

Naomi sat down on the bed next to Allison who was filing through a number of articles of clothing that were strewn across the bed.

"Hello, Baby. Mr. Raheleka has come. He sends his regards and will speak with you tomorrow."

"I could use some good news. I always enjoy conversing with him," Allison said with little enthusiasm.

"Having some difficulty?"

"Yes. Sophia."

"Sophia? What has *she* done?" Naomi asked.

Allison fidgeted with a blouse. "Only fell in love with an incredible man, married him, and is destined to live happily ever after."

"I detect a hint of resentment in your tone."

Allison tightened her lips, then exploded, "It is not fair, Mummy! Sophia is years younger and has not known Rahzvon nearly as long as I have known Guillaume...and Rahzvon is so..." She crunched up the blouse.

Naomi raised a brow. "I thought that you were quite content in your relationship with Guillaume?"

"I am...but God only knows when we will ever marry," she said spitefully.

"Are you ready to marry Guillaume?"

"Ready?" Allison left the bed, walked over, and closed a drawer in the wardrobe. "I am not sure."

"You have spoken of becoming his wife, many times. Has something changed your mind?"

Allison shrugged and sat down next to her mother.

Naomi took Allison's hand. "Perhaps in your observation of Rahzvon and Sophia, you have imagined what it would be like to be married to Guillaume. What did you mean when you said that Rahzvon was '*so*,' so what?"

Allison shrugged again.

"I think you know. Be honest with yourself."

Allison looked into her mother's comforting eyes. "Mummy, Rahzvon is handsome, strong, and in control. A woman would feel safe with him."

"A woman does," Naomi said worriedly.

Chapter VIII

"Broken Hearts"

"I shall not hear his voice complain,
But who shall stop the patient rain?
His tears must not disturb my heart,
But who shall change the years and part
The world from any thought of pain?"

—Alice Meynell

Allison left the bed. "I know, Mummy,—he loves Sophia, and I am happy for her...I think. But why does Guillaume have to be such a..."

"Guillaume is loving, quite attractive and very brave. He handled things well at the church with the gown ordeal. And have you forgotten the incident at Duncan Ridge with Ian and Dirth, or his display of courage in Kosdrev?"

"No," Allison mumbled.

"Look at me, Baby, and listen. There are few Rahzvons and Hirams in this world. Likewise, there are few women who belong with them. Indeed, they are very appealing in appearance and character. But by the same token there are few Guillaumes and Edwards, as well."

"Thank the Lord."

"*Allison,* that is not fair. Yes, they may make a few social bumbles, but they are truly loyal, devoted men who would lay down their lives for us. As for marrying, do not be so anxious to marry because someone else has. The time has to be right for both of you."

She placed her arm around Allison's shoulders. "I am going to say this because I am your mother. If you have feelings for Rahzvon, consider their source. He has shown you nothing but sincere friendship. Your attraction may only be for the man he represents. As for Guillaume, do not marry him out of boredom or because he is conveniently available. He is a wonderful, sensitive man who deserves nothing less than a woman who loves him with her whole heart."

Allison looked sheepishly.

"Baby, you have time—plenty. Have no doubts in your decision or you shall pay later. Now, I will leave you to your thoughts." She walked to the door.

"Mummy, may I ask you a very personal question?"

Naomi laughed a little. "You may ask...but I may not answer."

Allison approached her cautiously. "This is only an observation...do you still have feelings for Hiram?"

"*What?*" Naomi asked with astonishment.

"You brought his name up with Rahzvon's and I have taken note to your expression when he enters a room."

Naomi took Allison's hands in hers. "What you are witnessing is my concern for Hiram. I have been concerned for his welfare for most of my adult life. I have been with him at his worst—hurt and broken. It was unbearable; knowing that years of that pain was due to my negligence. Now, that Kade is gone, I have never been more thankful that he has Livia to love him. No, I can assure you that I love Edward, but Hiram will always hold a place in my heart...like a brother."

"I, too, feel so very sorry that he and Livia lost Kade. However, I do not think that I shall ever share a comfortable relationship with Hiram...considering my past with him."

"You were hurt. In time your anger towards him will fade and then you may join the masses who adore him," she said grinning. "Despite Hiram's social stature and financial reputation, I must inform you that he is but a sweet, uncommonly innocent little boy."

"Are we discussing the same man?"

Naomi smiled. "From my experience, all McDonnallys display a tough exterior, but have hearts made of glass." Naomi smiled.

***

Sophia's indecision over her attire delayed the Sierzik house hunt, which was scheduled to begin early that following morning.

"Rahzvon, look at me. I look ridiculous. This green frock makes me look like a pear."

He scratched his chin. "No, I cannot agree."

"No?" she pouted.

He walked around her. "No, definitely not a pear. I think a nicely shaped melon."

"Rahzvon!" She stomped her foot.

"What can you expect—you are no longer one— you are two."

She scowled.

"I am only teasing. One can barely tell that you are with child. You need to stop worrying about your appearance. You might as well face the truth; it will be awhile before you look like Anna Held, again. Besides, your negativity is not good for my son."

"Anna Held? Who is she?"

"Everyone knows Anna Held," he snickered.

"Oh, yes, of course...*Anna Held?* Then it hit her, "Son? Is that not a little pretentious of you?"

Rahzvon grimaced and whispered, "Presumptuous."

"It is of no consequence, *my daughter* may be offended by your presumptuousness," she said with her nose in the air.

He walked over and unhooked the chain to raise the table to the ceiling. "Phia, if that little baby is a girl, you may have to have me committed to an asylum," he laughed pulling the table upward. He secured it.

Sophia's glaring disapproval caught his eye. "But, I am certain that she will be as beautiful and as agreeable as her mother."

Sophia turned toward the mirror and stood

sideways. She removed a pin from her hair and replaced it. Rahzvon watched. Her self-admiration transformed into an expression of horror. She snapped around.

"Oh no! What if she has my bird nest hair every morning?"

He laughed, bent down and put his arms around her waist.

She rubbed her belly. "This is serious. Poor baby."

"Not to worry. You can braid her hair each night, while I am braiding yours." He kissed the top of her head.

She turned around in his arms and started to sniffle.

"*Phia*," he said tenderly.

"You—you are a positively perfect husband and father." She wiped a tear from her glistening eyes.

"I will do my best, but right now the three of us need a house large enough for us to sit in a row for the braiding. Shall we go? Mr. Fisher is waiting to show us our future home."

The Fisher home was a classic with a nicely landscaped lawn. It was definitely in "move in" condition and had distinct possibilities.

"I'll be returnin' to me shoe shop, now. You two stay as long as ye like. Just drop off the key when yer finished," Mr. Fisher instructed, climbing onto his horse.

"Thank you, sir. We would like to take some measurements before we make a decision," Rahzvon explained.

"Verra well, I'll be seein' ye. Like the preacher, I hae a cart load o' soles that need savin'," he chuckled as he rode off.

Sophia laughed, impressed by cobbler's humor. "Well, let us get on with the tour."

Rahzvon and Sophia entered the house. On completion, Sophia commented with noted despair, "It only has ten bedchambers."

"How many children do you think we are having? You McDonnallys. What are you—rabbits?"

"Not for the children—quarters for the guests and the servants."

"I said no servants."

"You said, no nanny."

"No nanny, no servants. I want my privacy."

"Then who do you expect to clean this mansion? It is enormous."

He took her hand, "Forget it. Come along, we are going to the Murphy's."

"But I like this house," she tugged from his grip.

"The Murphy house is smaller."

"*Smaller?*"

"Please, get into the carriage." Rahzvon helped her inside and instructed the coachman to drive to the cobbler's shop to return the key, before continuing on to the next prospect.

After a rather heated discussion on the steps of the Murphy house with Sophia, Rahzvon thanked the owner and explained, "Sir, I am afraid that we would not be interested; my wife prefers a home with windows to the west. Get in, Phia." His jaw tightened. They continued on.

"This one is lovely, Rahzie."

"Rahzie?" He grinned.

"Would you prefer, Vonnie?"

"No!"

Sophia pointed to an area to the east of the

house. "Look! It has a garden."

"The Fitzgeralds must be inside," he said helping Sophia down from the carriage. "Ah, here comes someone."

A tall, blonde man appeared in the porch and came out to meet them. His bright blue eyes were focused on Sophia. With a charming attentive smile he announced, "Welcome. I am Mr. Fitzgerald, but you may address me as Jerry."

"I am Sophia McDonnally." Sophia extended her hand, which Rahzvon immediately captured.

"*Sierzik*," Rahzvon corrected his smiling wife.

"Mr. and Mrs. Sierzik," Rahzvon said pointedly.

Jerry did not remove his gaze from Sophia while speaking to her annoyed husband.

"Mr. Sierzik, in regard to your recent correspondence—and the fact that you will be traveling quite often—well, I want you to rest assured that I will make a devoted effort in keeping an eye on Sophia and maintaining the grounds in your absence. I enjoy the exercise," he added, flexing his forearms. "I live in the stone cottage across the way. It would be my pleasure to oblige."

"That is awfully nice of—" Sophia began.

Rahzvon snatched hold of her hand again, and hustled her to the carriage as he called out, "Sorry, Mr. Fitzgerald—Jerry—but this house is entirely too small. We are planning a very large family—ten or twelve!" Rahzvon climbed in next to wide-eyed Sophia.

"Ten or twelve? But—"

"Never mind."

Sophia frowned. "Rahzvon, I loved that house. You did not give me the opportunity to see the interior."

"You have seen more than enough. We are going

to the house in the next village, outside of Langford. Albert suggested it." Still steaming from Jerry's transparent motives, Rahzvon mumbled under his breath, "The next village may not be far enough."

They rode two miles toward Langford, while Sophia continued to complain about their hasty exit from Jerry's house. Rahzvon fought to withhold further comment.

When they arrived, his attitude improved upon seeing the next estate. "Stop!" Rahzvon alerted the driver. "Look, Phia—a diamond in the rough!"

"Those look like animal houses. Keep driving!" she called out to the coachman.

"No!" Rahzvon ordered. "They are out buildings. I could raise our own livestock."

"Move on! I am in no condition to slop pigs, not that I would. On to the next one! That is ghastly."

Rahzvon gritted his teeth, "Move on to the next one!" he resigned.

The next residence in question looked agreeable enough on the exterior, but upon entry, the couple looked around, shook their heads in unison and made a quick exit for the carriage, while the family of rats shot toward the holes in the floorboards.

However, the house belonging to the widow McGuire seemed to be perfect.

"Rahzie, please come over here."

Rahzvon left the window where he was admiring the new shed.

Sophia was running her fingers across the satin brocade cushion. "It has a window seat, just like the one at home."

"We don't have a window seat."

"I mean at Uncle Hiram's. Look here—a built-in breakfront."

"Yes...look at that great tool shed." He pointed from the window. "What do you think? Shall we take it?"

"Should we not examine the upstairs, first?" Sophia looked at him dubiously.

"Of course. Now, mind your step. Hold the rail."

They entered the tastefully decorated corridor with periwinkle flowered wallpaper above the wainscot. Sophia moved through the hall, counting, "One, two, three, four—six bedrooms! Four for the children—I really think that four children—two girls and two boys would suffice. That would leave one for us and one for the nanny."

Rahzvon was staring out the window at the well-maintained barn to the south.

"Rahzie?"

"Yes, that is fine."

"A nanny?" she asked glowing.

"No—no!"

Sophia stuck out her bottom lip in a pout. "Fine, it will be the guest room." She fluttered off from room to room. "I love it! It is the house that I have always dreamed of owning!"

Back at the window, Rahzvon admired the acreage, imagining walking proudly across the small, but adequate estate. *Finally.* "I will notify Mrs. McGuire tomorrow!" he called back.

"No, no. We have to tell her today before she sells it to someone else."

"All right." Rahzvon laughed. He hugged her and led her back to the staircase.

"Stop," she said abruptly.

"What is it? The baby?" he asked with concern.

Sophia turned back to the bedrooms. "No, it is the baby's room—the nursery."

"What about it?" He followed her to the quaint

sunflower yellow room.

"Well, look at it—is it not obvious?" she asked with her hands resting on her hips.

"The color? We can paint it."

"No. The color is glorious. It is the location."

"I see no problem; it is directly across the hall from the master bedroom."

"Across the hall? Our helpless little baby is not sleeping all the way over there."

"Phia, it is only two steps." He took three very long strides to the doorway. "Well, only three."

"Your feet are much larger. For me it is..." She stepped it off. "Nearly seven. No, no, I shan't have it. This house will never do. An adjoining room for the baby is absolutely necessary. We shall have to keep looking." She started for the stairs.

"It can sleep in our—er...we can knock out a wall between the room next to it and put in a door," he offered, following her.

"It would never work. There would not be wall space for our furniture. It is out of the question." She took the rail and started down the steps.

"Phia, I *want* this house."

"Not to worry, we shall find another. We just have to continue searching."

"The search has ended. There are no other prospects. This was the last available property within the area," his voice escalated.

She turned at the bottom of the steps. "*I* liked the one with the view of the garden."

"So does *Jerry*. Forget it. We are going home," he grumbled.

"I do not want to go back to that little fish tin— take me to my uncle's," Sophia demanded. "My feet ache."

He helped her into the carriage. He froze.

Her condition is becoming more obvious. Eventually, Hiram is sure to notice.

Sophia entered her uncle's mansion with Rahzvon close on her heels. "Mr. Sierzik, you are the one who is unreasonable," she objected.

"I am unreasonable? I took you to every available house. This isn't the search for the Holy Grail; we simply need a house with room to walk. "

"Well, Sir Galahad, your search has ended, I choose this one." She plopped down on the divan in the parlor.

"Do you care to explain that threat?"

"*Simply*, I have chosen this one—Uncle Hiram's. He offered us the east wing," she announced sharply.

"First of all, I do not appreciate your ungrateful attitude and secondly, you refused the Murphy house because it did *not* have a western exposure."

"The bedroom was too small for my wardrobe," she said nonchalantly, slipping off her shoes.

He stepped in front of her. With one hand on his hip and his other shaking a finger at her, he laid down the law.

"Phia, you may be wealthy, but you are not the Duchess of Manchester. I can pay my own way and yours, as well. We are not living in the same house with your uncle. I shall not stand for him lording over me like a warden, constantly reminding me of my failures."

"Is that so?" She gave a mischievous grin and a giggle.

Rahzvon felt the strong clamp on his shoulder.

"Aye, Rahzvon?" Hiram inquired.

Rahzvon shook his head and walked away.

***

Thoroughly frustrated and defeated. Rahzvon spent the next three days rearranging the furniture in the eight rooms of the manor's east wing.

That following weekend, Naomi and Edward hosted a family gathering, as Pearl, her sister-in-law, was visiting with her sons. Naomi's brother, Jeremiah was on a business trip in Glasgow. Naomi's nephew, young Marvin, a natural-born city-dweller, found his visits to Lochmoor Glen to be nothing less than magical and intriguing.

The afternoon of the picnic, while watching Marvin patiently tend his fishing rod, Hiram recalled the many fishing excursions with Edward. Since the activity on the line was infrequent, Marvin traversed the water's edge in search of unusual stones and anything that moved. Hiram, who was lying on the overlooking bank, sat up when the boy squatted down and picked something up. He turned to Hiram and displayed that which would warm the heart of any lad who slept embracing a yard long corduroy replica of one of nature's most amazing creatures— the grass snake.

Hiram grinned while Marvin held the pencil-thin tail before him. The boy's eyes danced with delight as he studied the confused reptile, which coiled its upper body in a defensive posture. The tiny forked tongue shot out intermittently. Marvin moved through the crowd, thrilled to introduce his new pet to the family. He was quick to discover that the women were a bit squeamish and apprehensive with his aggressive approach, but Hiram applauded his find.

"Nice specimen, Marvin. We do not see many of them in Scotland. Take care to not pick up an adder, next time."

"I know, sir; they are venomous. We have grass snakes, like this one, in England."

The adults chatted and engaged in various lawn games as the hours sped by. When Livia left Hiram to speak with Pearl about her school, he saw Marvin crawling behind his newest companion and later carrying it. Hiram grinned when he heard him addressing it softly, "You are a good boy."

Marvin occasionally would give the reptile some relief from the summer sun with a quick dip in the pond before continuing their play. He observed the snake's every move when it was presented with a new line of obstacles, be it through tall grass or over stones. But not for one minute did Marvin give the foot-long captive the opportunity to escape. It soon became more relaxed and complacent. Wrapped around his wrist, Marvin carried it over to his grandmother, Beatrice. He then made an unexpected comment, which Hiram overheard.

Marvin pointed out his wonderful discovery, "Look, he has brown eyes like mine."

Hiram's heart skipped a beat—Kade and his dark McDonnally eyes flashed before him. He shuddered and looked away. Then Marvin shot past him to the shore and held his prize snake up for Rahzvon and Sophia to view from the opposite bank. Marvin returned downcast and reported to Hiram. "I don't think they saw him."

Marvin then ran off to continue the adventure with his extraordinary friend.

The time was too short before the captivated boy heard the dreaded words, "Marvin it is time to go into the house—put the snake down!" Beatrice called.

Now, Marvin, advised to release it several times

throughout the day, could not. Likewise, it made no impression on the boy when it was suggested that the snake might have family waiting.

"I want to take it home," he persisted.

"No, Marvin. This is where he lives," Beatrice explained.

"But I always wanted a snake," he stated matter-of-factly.

"Marvin, it may not eat if you were to take it and it would die."

"I will feed it."

"No, I am afraid that it needs to stay here by the pond."

Hiram shared Marvin's mounting tension—the fear of losing his beloved charge—the pain of letting go. Marvin stood helpless. Hiram could offer no advice to the child whose dream was coming to an end. He felt the need to say something to comfort Marvin, but how could he. He knew that making the sacrifice was unbearable. There were no words that could compensate for the void. There were no words to rationalize the injustice.

Hiram watched Marvin carefully lower his friend-for-a-day down next to the water.

"Perhaps, you will see him again, when you return," his grandmother offered.

"No, I shan't," Marvin said disdainfully and walked away.

No, you shan't. Hiram's anger surfaced, as well, knowing that he, too, would never see Kade again. How could he bear seeing Kade as another man's son?

Hiram watched the despondent little boy move slowly across the meadow. Empathetic, Hiram was soon walking next to him. He placed a hand on Marvin's shoulder. Marvin said nothing, but reached for Hiram's hand. Together they walked up the hill toward the house.

Livia watched from the bank.

The next morning Livia found Hiram sitting in his study. When she entered, he offered no greeting. It was time. She needed to open up to him about Kade. She took the chair across from him.

"I love you, Hiram."

He did not look up.

"I am hurting, angry and confused, too. It all seems to be a bad dream from which we cannot awaken. It does not seem possible." She left her chair and approached him. "Hiram, no matter how unbearable, we have to realize that we were given a rare opportunity. We were parents. We know the joy and responsibility of having a child. Rahzvon and Sophia, do, as well. Kade..."

Hiram's lowered head turned away.

Livia continued, "Yes, 'Kade.' We need to speak his name, darling. He may never know it, but during the time in which he lost his family and needed love and a nurturing home—we were there to give it to him. We were chosen to provide for him."

She took his hands in hers. "We cannot dishonor that blessing with anger and regret. Darling, can you even imagine having never known or loved Kade?"

Hiram raised his head. His eyes welled up. He got up and left the room. Livia did not follow him.

Later that week, after donning positions on three of the bedroom walls in the east wing, Sophia's monstrous vanity was placed on the fourth by Rahzvon and his discontent aids—Miles, Albert, and Gaelon. After recovering from the arduous task,

Rahzvon took refuge in his old residence in the barn, while Sophia was having tea with Livia. He threw down a bale and shoved it under the window where he had slept for months. Although he was satisfied that he had taken responsibility in moving the furniture, he loathed the housing situation. He sat, rubbing his forehead. Not only had he failed to provide a home for his family, but he had brought Sophia back into the McDonnally fold. His brow wrinkled at the disturbing reality. This could not continue. He looked out the window to that of Hiram's bedchamber.

Thoughts of Avera's note returned—what did it mean? The countless times that he read it, engraved the words upon his memory. *But which McDonnally was responsible?* He questioned how it was possible that it could be Hiram; he had been so gentle with Kade. But if Hiram was responsible, how could he and Sophia dare raise their child in the home of a criminal? Rahzvon closed his eyes in frustration and then went to find Hiram.

Chapter IX

"Numerous"

"You smiled, you spoke and I believed,
By every word and smile deceived."

—Walter Savage Landor

Rahzvon found Hiram standing at the doorway to the kitchen and addressed him without stopping. "Sir, I need to speak with you in your study."

Not accustomed to responding to Rahzvon's beck and call, Hiram hesitated as Rahzvon continued down the corridor. Hiram ran his hand across his beard and then followed. He entered the room, where he found Rahzvon standing by the fireplace and rubbing his chin nervously. Hiram closed the doors behind him. He took the chair across from Rahzvon and waited for the anxious young man to speak.

"Please, have a seat, Mr. Sierzik."

Rahzvon took the chair across from him and glanced up momentarily, avoiding the intimidating McDonnally gaze. "Sir—"

"Rahzvon, you may use my given name,"

"Hiram." He straightened in his chair. "Hiram, I think that you should know that although I am grateful for your offer to share your home with us, I find the arrangement to be unacceptable."

"I am well aware of that fact."

Rahzvon shifted. "A man needs his own home. I tried to find one, but your niece is so blasted stubborn and *koribil.*"

"Sophia, pig-headed?" he laughed. "Sophia is a McDonnally. You knew that when you married her."

Rahzvon left his chair. "Frankly, sir—Hiram, with no disrespect, might I remind you that she is a Sierzik, now, and needs to behave like one."

Hiram threw back his head and laughed again until he saw Rahzvon's face redden with disapproval. Hiram gained control and asked in a serious tone, "How do you plan to achieve that feat?"

"I need to get her out of this house and in my charge."

"Are you are implying that the members of my clan are a bad influence on my niece?"

"*My wife.*"

"Do you actually believe that Sophia will miraculously transform into a calm, rational well-tempered Sierzik, if you imprison her in that cigar box?"

Hiram's free use of the term "imprison" threw Rahzvon off balance, reminding him of the cryptic letter. The distraction and concern was apparent in his expression.

Hiram interpreted it, otherwise. "It would appear that you have taken a fall from your horse, so to speak. A single fall should not discourage one from riding again. Back into the saddle, Mr. Sierzik."

Rahzvon listened curiously.

Hiram got up and began to pace. "It is clear that you do not approve of living under another man's roof, nor do you condone your wife answering to another man's expectations—be it mine or anyone else's. Thus, I expect that these living arrangements to be temporary, at most. Now, what is it that you wanted to discuss? Are there other furnishings that you shall be needing? I have instructed Miles to pick up catalogues from the mercantile to give to Sophia. She may choose any additional furniture and have it billed to my account."

Rahzvon raised his head with noted contempt for his gracious benefactor and stood up face-to-face with him.

"No, Hiram. From now on, I shall be the one to provide for my family. Excuse me." Rahzvon left the study without another word, determined to honor that pledge.

Hiram, on the other hand, was quite pleased. "Aye, I thought that offer would toss you back in the saddle," he mumbled. Reviewing the conversation, Hiram wandered down the hall to the kitchen where he found Eloise chopping an onion for a stew. Feeling Hiram's presence, as he was leaning on the doorjamb, she turned and wiped the tears with her apron hem.

"Sir, were you in need of something?" she asked.

Hiram walked over to the table, picked up another onion and grinned. "Perhaps, onions were never meant for eating. What are you making?"

"An Irish stew for Daniel and Beatrice. Miss Nichols invited them to dinner."

"Aye." He replaced the onion into the basket. "Eloise, there is a grand old desk in the storeroom on the fourth floor. There is also a matching chair. Please have Albert deliver them to the east wing for Rahzvon."

"Yes, sir. Albert is in the garden. I will notify him at once." She wiped her tearing eyes again.

"Eloise, you need not weep over it, although it will add to your dusting duties." He smiled and winked at her.

"Oh, master," she laughed. She thought how nice it was to see Hiram smiling and making jokes, again. Perhaps, he was getting on with his life without Kade. "I have interviewed a few candidates for the new butler to assist Miles, sir."

"Very good, Eloise. I can always count on you."

In the garden, Sophia and Livia conversed over a tray of an assortment of berry tarts and scones.

"I just cannot decide which to have next. They all look so very delicious," Sophia said eying the afters. "Livia, do you know Anna Held?"

"Not personally. Why do you ask?"

"Earlier, Rahzvon made reference to her. How do

you think that I compare to her?"

"Well, you are both married—she to Mr. Ziegfeld, you to Rahzvon.

"Mr. Ziegfeld? Anything else?"

"She is a famous actress and..." Livia was at a loss.

"How would you say we compare in appearance?"

"Well, Sophia, that ridiculous eighteen inch waist, of which she boasts is comparable to no woman's." Livia shook her head.

"Eighteen inch waist! I have not had a waist that small since my first birthday!"

Livia laughed.

"That is absurd. Why her? Why could he have not compared me to another actress—say, Maude Adams?" she pouted, naming the actress.

Then Livia and Sophia's thoughts meshed. They smiled at one another and in there tiniest voices, in unison, repeated Miss Adams' famous line from Peter Pan, "Do *you* believe in fairies?" They broke into laughter again and then shouted together, "Yes!"

When they stopped laughing, Sophia ate another bite of her scone and then blotted her mouth with her napkin. "Forget Maude, I really see myself as," she lowered her voice to a sultry, throaty sound, "more the Ethyl Barrymore type."

Livia giggled. "Very good."

"I thank you. Now, Livia, *you* are more like Julia Marlowe," Sophia chose a tart.

"You see *me* as a Shakespearean actress? But, I have never performed in any of his plays. I doubt that I could memorize the lines."

Sophia swallowed and nodded. "It has been said that Julia was 'not only as lovely as Juliet, she was Juliet'," she stated with authority. "You would be the perfect Juliet, Livia."

"I am not certain of that, but I appreciate the compliment, Mrs. Sierzik." Livia nodded graciously.

Sophia placed her napkin in her lap. "With each passing day, I, unfortunately, look more and more like a dirigible. I would fear that I may float away at any minute, if it were not for all this weight."

"Well, I think that your condition only heightens your beauty. You would make the fans of Maxine Elliot sit up and take notice."

"*Livia*," Sophia said sheepishly.

"Yes, with those McDonnally eyes, Whistler would have surely christened you 'the girl with the midnight eyes,' instead of her."

Sophia stood up and gave an awkward curtsy. "I guess I had better abandon our meeting of the mutual admiration society and go take a nap."

Livia took her hand, "Sophia, it will go quickly and thank you for confiding in me."

"I had to tell someone about my baby. I am waiting to tell Mother, when Rahzvon tells Uncle Hiram, but at this rate, our baby may tell Uncle Hiram, before her father gets up the nerve."

Livia forced a smile. The mention of Hiram was making her uncomfortable. Things were still not quite right with him. Livia quickly changed the subject, "It has been wonderful chatting with you. I only wish that I could have had a relationship as agreeable with my sister."

"Well, you have me, now. There is obviously plenty to go around," she giggled.

"I shall see you at dinner."

"No doubt about that!"

"Good afternoon, Sophia." Livia saw Hiram entering the backdoor. *I miss him.* With that thought, she set out to talk to him.

***

Hiram entered the hall where he met his beaming servant. "Sir, there is a Miss Carlson waiting for you in the parlor. She desires to speak with you."

"Thank you." Hiram straightened his collar and proceeded to meet with her. *Miss Carlson?*

Rahzvon stood above them on the landing, curious, too, about the visitor, but continued toward the east wing. Livia entered the backdoor and headed for the parlor.

"Good morning, Mr. McDonnally, I am pleased to make your acquaintance. Hester Carlson, sir."

Livia stood just outside the parlor, deterred from entering by the woman's voice.

"Welcome, Mrs. Carlson."

"*Miss* Carlson, sir."

"I beg your pardon. What may I ask brings you to Lochmoor Glen and more specifically to my home, Miss Carlson?"

"You, sir."

Livia remained concealed—not at all thrilled by the woman's reply.

"Mr. McDonnally, are you not one of Britain's greatest financiers?" Hester asked.

Hiram gave a little laugh, "That remains to be seen in light of the recent conflict abroad."

"Shall we sit, I have been traveling a great distance."

"Oh, again, I beg your pardon. Please have a seat."

"Come sit next to me. What a lovely divan."

Next to her? Livia mentally objected.

"Hiram, may I call you Hiram?" Hester asked.

"Certainly."

"I believe in being honest in expressing my

opinions. Your uncommon appearance lends itself to *numerous* compliments. My father had a beard, too."

Livia got down on the floor and peeked around the corner of the archway to see the thin, blonde-haired woman fawning over Hiram.

"Miss, I thank you, but exactly what may I do for you?"

Livia's stomach churned miserably at his inquiry.

"*Numerous* things, I am certain...but one in particular has drawn me to your doorstep. I am a novice, an involuntary student of commerce, thrown into the financial world by the unexpected and heartbreaking death of my father."

Carlson? "You are the daughter of H.T. Carlson?" Hiram said with apparent shock.

"I am—in the flesh."

Livia watched Hiram sit up and take notice. Livia was poised to pounce.

"This is a great honor, Miss Carlson. Your father was a genius."

"I agree whole-heartedly, but in this case, unfortunately, the apple has fallen far from the tree. I am helpless in these matters. That is my purpose for this visit. I feel that no other man is qualified to advise me. Your references are *numerous*."

Numerous? Is that the only adjective she knows? Livia thought, rolling her eyes upward. *Qualified, extraordinarily handsome, and unmarried. She is as transparent as that veil she was wearing.*

"Miss Carlson—"

"Please, *Hester*."

"Hester, your vote of confidence is greatly appreciated, I assure you. However, I am faced with a horde of decisions of my own—having connections in both Austria and Berlin."

"Perfect. We could work them out together—form an alliance."

Hiram left the divan in disbelief. His quick response floored Livia.

"Miss Carlson, I am awed by your proposal. Come join me in my study. There we can speak privately." He offered her his arm.

That was the last straw. Livia scrambled to her feet, fled directly to the study. She sat breathless in the nook behind the bookcase, which divided the room.

Miss Carlson entered and walked to the window. "Hiram, I must say that I am surprised at this arrangement."

"I beg your pardon?"

"The desk in front of the window. Do you not find it to be terribly distracting?"

"Uh...aye. The housekeeper had moved it. For years, I had it over here—" he stopped short in hearing a cough emanating from the nook. He stepped beyond the bookcase and swallowed hard. "Miss Carlson, may I introduce...a...a dear friend of mine, Miss Livia Nichols? Livia, Miss Carlson."

Livia stood and offered a sweet smile, "Miss Carlson." Livia withheld the desired glare for her *friend,* Hiram.

"My pleasure, Miss Nichols, I am honored to meet any of Hiram's numerous friends."

Hiram smiled nervously. Livia was challenged to maintain her sweet demeanor, but managed.

"Very well then, Miss Nichols, Miss Carlson and I shall be engaged in several hours of conference, so I shall see you at dinner." Hiram quickly took Livia's hand, offered a tight-lipped smile, and led her to the hall. She said nothing and hurried up the stairs.

Moving at a steady pace down the corridor, Livia

entered her bedroom, fell to her bed where she buried her face in her pillow, and let out a muffled scream.

She raised her head to a tap at the door. "Ah, finally," she sighed. "You see the error in your ways."

She scooted off the bed, primped her hair and hurried to greet Hiram. However, the man on the opposite side of the door was not her contrite beau, but the discontent Mr. Sierzik.

"Hello, Rahzvon."

"Livia, I need to speak with you. Would you care to walk with me in the garden?"

"Of course." Livia looked down the vacant hall, hoping to see Hiram and sighed.

Passing through the maze of shrubs, Rahzvon asked Livia , "Why is Miss Carlson paying a visit?"

"She claims to need Hiram's financial assistance."

"Oh? I wonder if Gaelon is aware of this. He has spoken vaguely of an indifferent acquaintance with her."

Livia's brows knitted.

Preoccupied with his displeasure in sharing a home with Hiram, Rahzvon changed the subject and presented his problem, "Livia, this arrangement is very disturbing."

"I agree, one-hundred percent," Livia quickly responded, believing Rahzvon to be speaking of Hiram's new business arrangement with the obnoxious Miss Carlson.

"You do?"

"Absolutely, Rahzvon."

"At last, an ally. What can we do about it? Any suggestions?"

"I think that we need to get her out of this

house," Livia said adamantly.

"I am certain of that," Rahzvon ran his fingers back through his hair, "but, she adores Hiram and this house."

"This house? *My* house?"

"Well, Livia, I have to agree. You know what they say about two women living under the same roof."

Livia tightened her lips.

"For all concerned, the sooner she is content to leave—the better," Rahzvon added fervently.

"I believe she adores his beard," Livia mumbled remembering Miss Carlson's remarks.

"Do you think that I should grow one?" Rahzvon asked hoping to please Sophia.

"No, no! Definitely not. We have enough problems with her attraction to Hiram's."

Rahzvon looked at her inquisitively, "I suppose you know best—being a woman."

Livia turned to her escort and looked up at him with a keen expression. "Rahzvon, we should work together on this."

Rahzvon nodded. "I agree. You know Hiram better than I."

"The financial arrangement is our greatest problem—she believes that she cannot survive without Hiram," Livia said folding her hands.

"Believe me, I am aware of that. There is no doubt that she believes that the sun rises and sets with his command," Rahzvon gestured an offer to sit on the concrete bench.

Livia sat down, pondering the dilemma. A broad, but serene smile soon spread across her face. "Well, it is time that she learned otherwise. When I am finished, her confidence in his financial expertise will be obliterated."

"You won't go too far, Livia? I do not want Hiram

throwing us out."

"No, not to worry. Can you just make certain that she joins us for dinner. I do not want to appear too obvious."

"No, problem there." Rahzvon smiled with new hope of escaping the confines of "Hiram's castle" and finding his own.

"Good. Leave the rest to me," Livia said confidently, standing and smoothing her skirt.

Rahzvon offered his arm. "It is a pact."

"A pact."

Chapter X

"Father says—"

"But lest your kissing should be spoiled
Your onions must be fully boiled."

—Jonathon Swift

That evening, at the dinner table, Rahzvon winked at Livia denoting his success in luring Sophia to the dinner table—a feat that required absolutely no encouragement on his part. Livia, on the other hand, accepted his signal with a grateful smile, believing him to have kept his promise of insuring Miss Carlson's attendance—unaware that Hiram was responsible for the invitation.

Livia wasted no time in implementing her plan of action. She smiled confidently at her nemesis and then addressed Hiram, "May I ask how your meeting fared?"

"Livy, thank you for asking. Quite satisfactory. Do you not agree, Miss Carlson?"

"Splendid, on *numerous* accounts. Mr. McDonnally is quite assuredly, an expert in his field."

Expert in his field? This comment temporarily sidetracked Livia, as it was Hiram's former description of his kissing abilities. She glanced at the other diners nervously. Rahzvon's demanding stare soon snapped her back to the task at hand and she proceeded with a vengeance. "Yes, Hiram does enjoy handling money," she laughed. "I mean working with capital."

Hiram half-smiled.

Livia continued, "Now, I, for one, know nothing about money matters, however, I found it to be uncommonly generous of Mr. McDonnally to invest so much revenue in the tiny Kosdreven fleet." She placed a piece of chicken on her plate.

"Well—" Hiram began to explain modestly, but Livia cut him off.

"So much money—such a tiny country. But I hear she is incredibly beautiful."

"The country?" Miss Carlson asked.

"Oh, no—Princess Creazna of Kosdrev. Do you not agree, Rahzvon?" Livia turned to Hester, "He is a Kosdrevian."

Rahzvon sat up ready to aid in the attack to undermine Hiram's character. "Yes, I agree, she is quite beaut—" He was stopped short by a sharp warning pain in his shin from his disapproving wife. "Ah, yes, he paid an exorbitant sum. Ours is such a tiny insignificant country."

Hester turned to Hiram with concern, "Hiram, where is this Korsev?"

"*Kosdrev*," Hiram corrected.

Rahzvon chimed in, "It is a rugged 'wee' country, as the Scots would say, situated near the mountain range in Norway. Too small to be on any map, though." Rahzvon winked at Livia. "But we are a fine strong people," he added, smiling at Hester.

Sophia gave Rahzvon another reminding kick.

Hester questioned skeptically, "Hiram, is this true? You, invested in a fleet of a nameless country?"

Before Hiram could reply, Rahzvon reiterated, "Kosdrev."

Hiram sat up taller. "I assure you, Miss Carlson, that transaction was an act of compassion and necessity."

"Compassion for the princess?" Hester scowled.

Livia moved in for the kill, "Oh yes. Hiram is renowned for his acts of generosity. I would wager that he was too modest to tell you that he financed the village schoolhouse."

Hiram sighed and smiled.

Rahzvon added, "Which burnt to the ground." He raised a questioning brow to Sophia.

Hiram's eyes widened.

Livia continued, "Mr. McDonnally has also offered to purchase everything that I need for my teaching facility."

"I was not aware that you were a teacher, Miss Nichols," Hester said curiously.

Livia looked up from her plate, dabbed her mouth and smiled sheepishly. "I am not a teacher... actually, I have had no formal training whatsoever, but I adore children. Mr. McDonnally felt that money was no object and I could choose whatever I desired to outfit my facility." Livia threw Hiram a quick innocent smile.

Obviously disenchanted with Hiram's financial priorities, Hester dropped her napkin onto the table and stood up. "If you will excuse me, I really should be returning to London."

"Please, finish your meal," Hiram insisted.

"Mr. McDonnally, I thank you for your hospitality. You have educated me on numerous topics, but for the time being, I think that I shall refrain from any final decision on a merger."

Hiram left his chair, "Certainly. Perhaps, we could we take some time to discuss this privately?"

Livia's heart stopped.

"I think not," Hester said leaving the room.

Livia lowered her head to hide her victorious grin. She glanced up and met Hiram's suspicious glare, which then moved directly to challenge her accomplice, Rahzvon.

"May I escort you to your carriage, Miss Carlson?" Hiram offered.

"That shan't be necessary. The butler will suffice."

"Very well, I will ring for Miles."

While doing so, Rahzvon whispered to Sophia, "Miss Carlson was not too impressed with your uncle."

Sophia sat down her fork and said in a low tone,

"She is a fool. She knows nothing. Uncle Hiram is ten times the man her father was."

Ten times—that is questionable, Rahzvon thought considering Hiram's possible involvement with Avera, the author of the condemning note. He sat back, disappointed at having not made any headway with Sophia and surprised that she was familiar with Carlson Industries. He gave Livia a look of defeat; Sophia was not at all affected by the scheme to denigrate Hiram. She was not moving anywhere—content to reside in the McDonnally mansion for all eternity. However, Livia seemed pleased with the outcome, which confused Rahzvon.

Hiram returned to the head of the table. Livia's smile faded with two harsh words, "Saboteurs pay." He turned to Eloise, clearing away the plates, "That matter about the items in the attic—take them back," he demanded, feeling that Rahzvon's behavior was undeserving of the desk and chair, he had so generously offered.

"Yes, sir."

Hiram completed his dinner in silence; Livia dared not speak. Sophia's only interest was the tray of delectable afters. Rahzvon felt the impending doom of spending the rest of his life in the east wing. He knew, now, that any chance of even being thrown out was remote, at best; Hiram would prefer to "make him pay"—under his thumb.

Still focused on his goblet, Hiram swallowed his last sip of drink and announced. "Miss Nichols, your presence in the study would be greatly appreciated."

Miss Nichols? A twang of fear shot through her veins, but she responded instantly, "I do not recall leaving any presents in the study."

Hiram turned to her and raised his right brow just in time to see her innocent smile and shrug for the pun.

Sophia, unable to contain herself, burst into laughter over Livia's quick comeback and choked on her berry biscuit. Rahzvon patted Sophia's back, yet feared for Livia.

Hiram assisted Livia with her chair and pointed toward the hall. Livia, praying silently for guidance, made a sharp turn to the right into the parlor where, hopefully, Hiram would restrain his temper. However, a quick grasp to her left hand diverted her path to the dreaded study. By the time he had clapped the doors together, Livia was standing upon the window seat.

He stepped over, looked eye-to-eye with her and asked, "What are you doing up there?"

"I am establishing my position," her voice wavered.

"Position for what—further attack?"

"My defense. My father said to always establish your position and stand firm."

"He did, did he? And what did your father say in regard to interfering in business transactions of which are none of your concern?"

"He said that all business transactions *were* of his concern."

Hiram narrowed his eyes at her insolence.

"Now, Mr. McDonnally, with that discussion ended, would you care to help me down?" she asked sweetly.

Hiram declined, lowered his head, and gave a little chuckle. He walked behind his desk, sat down, leaned back, and raised his feet to rest upon it. "Nay, I think that I prefer you 'establishing your position' where I can view you with astonishment. There are no words to describe you, Livia Nichols. One minute you're a desk ornament—another you are ranting from your soap box."

"No words? I know of many words to describe you, Hiram McDonnally. Not too *numerous* to mention: handsome, powerful, intelligent, generous, tolerant, loving, understanding, *forgiving*—should I continue?"

Hiram shook his head, "It is not going to work, Livy."

"Are you denying these truths, Master McDonnally?"

He lowered his feet and scooted closer to the desk. He lifted a paperweight and slid it back and forth, intensely staring at it. He raised his head, "Livy, why? Nay, I know why." He held the paperweight and spoke, "Hard times are ahead. That alliance with Carlson Industries may have been the only saving factor for the McDonnally investments."

Livia turned uncomfortably away, toward the window.

"Livy, please turn around when I am speaking with you."

"Are you going to pitch that paperweight at me?" she asked pitifully.

"Livy, why do you say such ridiculous things? Now, please turn around. Have a go at it—offer your defense. I am extremely curious as to how you can rationalize your behavior."

Livia pivoted to face him and cleared her throat. "I have a sense about people. I feel that she would not have been a good business partner."

"Perhaps, I should invite all my associates for your scrutiny, so that you may eliminate those that you *feel* are detrimental to my dealings," he said sharply. "On what basis did you form this opinion of Miss Carlson—intuition alone, or jealousy?"

"Hiram, she openly criticized me in my very own

home!"

"*Your* home?" he cocked his head curiously.

Livia gasped. Her heart stopped. It was as though the very breath had been knocked out of her. Her eyes welled up, she squatted down, and stepped from the window seat. Once again, it happened ever so quickly. She fled to the doors. She was gone in a flash and left Hiram with his foot in his mouth.

"She did it again; she made me say the wrong thing! I have no control with that lass. How does she do it? I always end up in the wrong," he growled and grabbed a vase, ready to pitch it to the floor. He stared at it, returned it to the table and stepped over to the doorway. He leaned against the doorjamb. He could not be angry with her. Livia's talents were unmatched and nothing less than ingenious. He addressed the silent room, "I am definitely marrying that woman." He left to find her and met Rahzvon and Sophia in the hall.

"Uncle Hiram—" Sophia began, when Hiram gestured with a brushing motion.

"Off—go, go to the east wing!"

Sophia, with narrowed eyes, took Rahzvon's arm and announced, "If you are looking for Livia, she left through the back door."

Hiram continued to the rear entrance where he saw Livia running toward the barn. His ego curbed his instincts to chase after her. He casually trailed her.

In the barn, a quick check of the empty stalls produced no evidence of her. "She must be outside," he whispered, but a slight rustling in the loft sent him up the ladder. Crawling beneath the low rafters, he inched toward her. Livia's face was dirty and tear-streaked. He sat next to her, took her hand, raised it to his lips and kissed it.

"I am a fool, Livy, and you are entirely too sensitive."

"Ah!" She moved away from him.

Hiram moved closer. "If I had our toad, I would sit it beside you. I would tell you how he confided that he adored living with you in *your* new home."

Livia sniffled. Hiram looked around helplessly, lacking the necessary words to right his wrong, and surrounded by nothing but straw. Finally, he picked up a few pieces of straw and twisted them together to fashion a "T." He tapped Livia's wrist. "Good day, Mum. I am Master Strawman, spokesman for my friend toad."

Livia could not withhold a little giggle.

Encouraged, Hiram danced the little creation up her arm. "Toad told me that the master was never happier in your house, since you and toad came to live there at his—er, *your* estate."

Livia looked solemn again. Hiram pulled her into his arms. "Love, I sincerely apologize," he whispered, "of course it is your home, and it always shall be."

"Hiram, she was not a good prospect; besides, she adored your beard," Livia pouted.

"What?"

"Miss Carlson."

"*You* adore my beard. I am not, or ever will be interested in *her* opinion of my appearance."

"You introduced me as a *friend.*"

"Livy, you are my friend—my dearest friend. Would you have rather I said, 'this is Livia Nichols, my passion, my love, the reason for my very existence?'"

"Yes."

"Very well, when I see her at the meeting in town, I promise that I will elaborate on the state of our relationship."

"Meeting in London?" Livia pulled away.

Hiram tightened his hold on her. "Where ye goin' lassie?"

"Home."

"And where might that be?"

"*My* mansion."

"Ah—the perfect response. You m' lady have earned a kiss. Would you desire it here?" He pointed to her hand. "Or here?" He stroked her stained cheek. "It *is* rather dirty though," he said examining his finger.

"Is there an alternative?" she asked.

Hiram placed his hand behind her neck and drew her face close to his. "Hmm? There *is* an interesting place a bit below this enchanting nose. It appears to be rather inviting. Would that be acceptable?" he whispered in her ear.

She reached up and ran her fingers through his raven curls and then down to his beard. "I do not know if I desire to be kissed by such a financial incompetent."

Hiram sat back. "You are incorrigible, Livia Nichols."

"And you, sir, are either uncommonly shy or incredibly foolish."

"Do you dare qualify that statement?"

"How many men, in such an advantageous situation in the privacy of a loft, would ask for but one kiss, instead of dozen from a willing lady?"

"A dozen, you say? My darling, you are in the presence of a well-bred gentleman."

Livia pulled away, "Well, then there is no reason to loiter any longer." She scrambled toward the ladder.

Hiram grabbed a hold of her ankle. "Now wait a

minute!"

"Let go of me, you—you gentleman!" Livia screamed and laughed.

From below, the sound of someone clearing their throat instantly ended their play.

"I beg your pardon, Mr. McDonnally, but there is a guest waiting in the parlor," Miles announced and quickly left the barn.

Livia covered her mouth with her hand. Hiram grinned watching her face turn a pale pink. She swallowed then asked nervously, "Is Miles a gossip?"

"Not to worry—I shall double his pay this month."

"If it is that woman again with her numerous propositions—send her away! You had better go. I will wait a few minutes."

"A kiss, first, you hussy."

She gave him a quick peck on his forehead. "Please, Hiram, go quickly. I have never been so embarrassed."

Hiram started down the ladder. He climbed back up. "One. I deserve one, at the very least, for having to bribe Miles for his silence."

"You would as soon fire him as bribe him."

"True."

Livia rolled her eyes and crawled over to offer one very brief kiss.

"You call that a kiss?" he muttered on his way out of the barn. He turned and shook his finger at her. "I intend to collect later!"

"Shh!"

Livia turned to climb down when she paused and crawled back to where they had been sitting, and began searching through the straw. "There you are." She crawled back to the ladder with the little faux man, but a conversation below deterred her from continuing.

"Marvel, you hae better hae a good reason for draggin' me in here," Wilmoth grumbled. "I told Sophia that I would exercise Hunter for a full hour."

"Wilmoth, I saw somethin' and I hae to tell someone or I'll burst!"

Oh no, she saw Hiram and I up here, Livia thought.

"Get on wi' it, Marvel."

"Ye promise to keep a secret?"

Livia grimaced, above.

"Aye, make haste, I need to get back to Hunter. I hae to hurry to prepare for James' visit."

"Why do ye want to see that silly boy?"

"James is not silly—he is brilliant and Seth says that James thinks me to be quite bonnie."

"Ugh."

"I am leavin."

"Wilmoth, 'tis 'bout Master Rahzvon."

"Rahzvon?"

"Aye."

Rahzvon? Livia listened while Marvel explained.

"I was waitin' to show Miss Sophia the Girls Handy Book and—"

"And?"

"Well, I did and stop interruptin'. This is serious."

"Now, ye sound like Sophia."

"I saw him wit' a letter, Wilmoth!"

"What a shock," Wilmoth said sarcastically.

"Nay, a secret letter."

"*Marvel.*"

"I saw him in the mirror. He heard Sophia comin' in the room and he hid it in a drawer."

Livia swallowed hard.

"Marvel, 'tis Rahzvon's private affair. You hadna

right."

"But Wilmoth, he didna want Sophia to find it."

"'Twas probably a receipt for a gift."

"'Twas not. 'Tis a letter."

"You didna take it out o' the drawer?"

"I did."

"Well, what did it say? Was it from a woman?" Livia opened her eyes wide.

"Aye, maybe."

"And?"

"I didna read it—Sophia was comin' back into the room. I was nearly found out."

"Where is it, now?"

"I returned it to the back o' the drawer."

"Leave it be, Marvel Wheaton. Mama says letters are only for the eyes o' the addressee."

"What is a addressee?"

"*An* addressee—the recipient of the letter. Now, stay out o' the Sierziks' furniture—do ye promise? I'll tell Mama, if ye dunna forget it. I promise ye that!"

"But poor Sophia—"

"Marvel!"

Livia peeked over the edge of the loft and watched Wilmoth march her sister out of the barn. Livia sat debating the ethics of the situation. Trusting Marvel Wheaton to keep Rahzvon's secret was not an option. Livia had no choice. Although dreading the task, she knew that she had to warn Rahzvon of the little girl's knowledge, despite the contents of the letter in question.

Hiram gave a few swipes to his sleeves, paused at the hall mirror and removed a piece of straw from his hair. Having no clue to the identity of his guest he stepped into the archway with a greeting smile.

"Hello, Hiram," a nervous feminine voice spoke.

Speechless, he remained fixed in his position. She was the absolute last person he expected to find waiting for him. His confusion was apparent by his immobility.

"I knew that you would be surprised. You were never one to conceal your emotions. Please, come sit by me—here, Hiram." She tapped on the divan.

"I see the beard is back," she noted.

His hand moved slowly to his face and dropped. He walked slowly to the overstuffed chair by the fireplace as a lion tamer entering the beast's cage. He sat down.

"It feels grand to be back in Lochmoor Glen...and here in your parlor. Hiram, please, tell me that you are glad to see me, again."

"Have you come to visit your brother, Abby?"

Chapter XI

"Boomerang"

"Once fondly lov'd and still remember'd dear,
Sweet early object of my youthful vows,
Accept this mark of friendship,
Warm, sincere—Friendship!
'tis all cold duty now allows."

—Robert Burns

"Yes, Hiram, I have come to see Daniel, but that is not the sole purpose of my visit," Abigail replied in a composed manner.

He watched as she moved across the room towards the window. Her fingers slid over the familiar table and rocking chair as she passed. She turned to him.

"Remember the day that I arrived and Heidi frightened me?"

Hiram nodded.

Abigail sat on the window seat. "Do you also remember when you found me standing in the kitchen and you insisted that I pet her to overcome my fear?"

He hesitated and nodded again, curious as to where this one-sided conversation was leading.

"I have always been very independent and confident...but then there was the incident with Delilah's visit and the attack at Duncan—"

"Abby, some things are better to be left in the past."

"The point that I am trying, so pathetically, to make, is that you, Hiram, were there to reassure me in my every moment of weakness."

The insinuation was that Abigail had returned merely for further *reassurance*. However, Hiram found her presence to be very disquieting. Abigail's husband had not come with her and Livia was not far away. For the moment, Hiram felt vulnerable. Offering reassurance or anything else was not only undesirable, but he suspected to be quite possibly dangerous. He had made too many recent mistakes with Livia; their relationship may not stand up to yet another.

"Abby, where is your husband?"

Her unrelenting stare moved to the portrait of

Hiram's uniformed father above the mantle, then to her folded hands. She tightened her lips, seemingly fighting the tears, and began to tremble. Hiram's brows wrinkled. He panicked and left his chair and moved quickly to her side.

"Abby, what has happened? Please, tell me."

"I...I have left him." A tear trickled down her cheek.

Abigail was rarely moved to tears; he had seen her crying, only once—the day she was attacked on Duncan Ridge. It touched him deeply. He put a comforting arm around her and asked gently, "But why, Abby?"

She sniffled and wiped the tears away. "Roland is nothing like you, Hiram. He does not understand me."

Hiram stared blankly; this was not the response he had anticipated. His arm dropped slowly to the window seat while she explained further.

"He despises my brother. You adore Daniel. Roland is arrogant and self-centered." She nervously wiped the next few tears that escaped.

Hiram awkwardly brought his arm back around her and rocked her gently, in lieu of comforting words, which might strengthen her case.

She looked up at him with pleading eyes, "Hiram, I am so very sorry. I treated you horribly—with such disrespect. I have not known a moment of true happiness since the day that I left this room." She clutched his arm. "Everything was perfect—your proposal in the ditch, our truce in the library at Brachney Hall. I was incredibly foolish—I spoiled all of it—all of my dreams with the perfect man," she sobbed.

Abigail's confession, although relieving for her, brought unmarked anxiety to her attentive ex-fiancé.

If Hiram ever felt the need to flee, this was the moment. He had to nip this one in the bud, without a second's delay.

"Abby, no two men are alike. You cannot compare us—after all, the very reason that you left me was your disappointment in my character. Lattimer is a soldier. You cannot expect him to behave like a civilian." Hiram glanced at his father's portrait. "My father, although my own flesh and blood, was nothing remotely like me."

She snuggled into his chest. "I know and only now do I realize how impossible my marriage to Roland has become. I belong right here."

Hiram felt a deep-rooted pain forming in his stomach. He might as well have been on the front lines fighting for his life without a weapon. Being the pacifist that he was, he had to think quickly to insure his escape.

"Abby, have you discussed your feelings of discontent with him? Perhaps—"

Abby's head bobbed up. "Discussion? It was not! After he ordered me to silence, I told him. I gave him a piece of my mind!"

Hiram rolled his eyes upward in near hopeless surrender. "Aye, Abby, I am certain that you did," he mumbled.

She left the seat. "I told him that he was not one-tenth the man that *you* are!"

Hiram's memory shot back to the library scene with Abigail when she confessed that she had spoken the exact phrase to Ian MacGill.

"Abby, a man does not desire to be compared with another, especially being compared to... to his wife's old friend." The hazardous *'friend'* barely passed through his lips before she objected.

"Friend? Hiram, you asked me to marry you and

I accepted. We were betrothed!"

"But—"

She moved back into her clinging hold. "Hiram, I want to come home—home to McDonnally Manor, where I belong."

The *déjà vu* of the scene was too much for him. He was revisiting the heart-wrenching break-ups with Allison and Elizabeth Potter. *Why me? They leave me, then they return only after it is too late! Like boomerangs! I am always the antagonist!*

His heart pounded in his chest. Fearing that Abigail could hear it, he left her arms and walked to the center of the room, trying to get his bearings and control. "Abby, *you* broke our engagement. You called it off."

"I was confused by the uniform. I was angry— you know how moody I can be. But unlike Roland, you knew that ordering me around was unacceptable. Yes, Hiram, you know me. Roland nearly broke my spirit," she scorned.

"Abby, I..." He shook his head, walked to the hearth and stared into the dark cavern. *She was my spring spirit, but not anymore.*

"Sir, Excuse me, it is urgent—it is Miss Sophia!" Hiram looked up to see Eloise's distraught face. "Sir, Albert has gone for Dr. Lambert."

Hiram and Abigail ran with Eloise to the east wing where they found Sophia laying in bed with Rahzvon sitting next to her, holding her hand.

A cold chill fell over Hiram as he approached them. "What has happened?"

"Abigail," Sophia said grinning, "I am so happy to see you."

Abigail moved to the other side of the bed and kissed Sophia's forehead. "Hello, Sophia."

"Sophia, are you ill?" Hiram asked desperately.

"I think it is perfectly normal," Sophia said calmly.

"What is?" Hiram demanded in his frustration.

"My fainting. I fainted-dead away—right over there by my vanity. Is it not a glorious piece of furniture, Abigail?"

"It is—"

"Fainted?" Hiram cut Abigail off.

"Yes, Uncle Hiram. Women with child tend to do that."

Rahzvon froze, when once again he suddenly found himself airborne and pressed to the wall.

"Hiram!" Abigail screamed. "Stop!" She ran and grabbed his arms.

"You did this to her?!" Hiram shouted in Rahzvon's face.

With one heave, Rahzvon shoved Hiram back. "I am her husband!"

Sophia sat up. "Stop it, both of you! I want this baby and if you two continue, I *will* need a doctor."

Abigail tugged on Hiram's arm. "She is right, darling. Come along," she coaxed.

Livia stood by the doorway watching the unexpected scene unfold. Feeling nauseous, she questioned, *Abigail?* What was she doing here? *Darling?* Where was her husband? The gentle push from Sophia's concerned mother brought her back to the moment.

"Excuse me," Hannah said, darting toward her daughter. "Sophia?"

"I am fine, Mother," Sophia reassured her and then glared at Hiram.

Hannah followed her daughter's disapproving gaze toward her twin. "Hiram?" she inquired, seeing his face red with fury and Rahzvon breathing hard.

"Mama, Uncle Hiram, is not taking the news of

our baby, very well."

"Baby?" Hannah's jaw dropped.

"Yes, Mama, you are to be a grandmother in the spring," Sophia announced proudly, reaching out for Rahzvon's hand. He straightened his shirt and possessively grasped her hand, after throwing Hiram a reproachful warning.

"Sophia, I cannot believe it—you are so young." Hannah hugged her.

"Mother, you were much younger than I, when I was born."

"But you have been married for such a short time," she said stroking Sophia's hair. "Though, you have had some experience with babies with..." Hannah paused daring not to continue with mention of the absent orphan, Kade.

Hiram's face grew dark. He moved to the window with Abigail attached to his arm.

Feeling like an outsider, Livia remained in the shadows of the hall watching the McDonnally family event. She stepped back wondering how it was possible that *she*—the love of Hiram's life—was not involved—not even missed. Yet, Abigail O'Leardon, specter from his past, was there consoling him in the thick of it. Livia felt another gentle nudge—this time from Dr. Lambert.

"Excuse me, miss," he said fumbling with his pocket watch.

Other than Hannah and the doctor, Rahzvon was the only one who noticed Livia's presence. He watched with concern as she fled down the hallway when the doctor instructed that the room be vacated while he examined Sophia.

Still seething, Rahzvon waited for Hiram to enter the corridor. He would show him no mercy. Seeing Hiram with Abigail had only heightened his rage. Rahzvon adored Livia and could only imagine her pain. She had lost Kade and needed Hiram more than ever.

"Hiram, I want to speak with you," Rahzvon demanded with a tone that caused Hiram to pull his arm from Abigail's grasp.

Rahzvon nodded for Abigail to move on. She did, however, reluctantly.

Rahzvon stepped up directly into Hiram's face. "A word of warning—never upset my wife again! And one question—what *kind* of man are you? You parade around with one woman on your arm to break the heart of another—a woman of the sweetest, gentlest, disposition of any on earth? You disgust me."

Reference to Livia immediately extinguished Hiram's oncoming rage. He turned quickly toward the opposite end of the hall where Abigail approached the staircase.

He grabbed Rahzvon's arm, which Rahzvon immediately jerked free. "Livia was here?" Hiram panicked.

"Had you not been so preoccupied with Miss O'Leardon and attacking me, you would have seen Livia watching from the doorway. I never thought I would say this, but it is apparent to me that she deserves much better than you, *Master* McDonnally."

Rahzvon stepped over to the opposite wall.

Hiram thought for a second. "Rahzvon, please inform me as to Sophia's condition, as soon as you hear."

Rahzvon said nothing. Hiram shot down the hall and addressed Abigail in passing. "I shall speak with you in the parlor...later."

He descended the stairs and ran through the maze of corridors leading to Livia's room where he pounded on the door.

"Livy, open this door!"

Not waiting for her response, he flung it open. The room was vacant. A quick scan verified that her things were still there. *She hasn't left.* He ran downstairs to the parlor, study, dining room and kitchen. He sprinted to the west wing, which produced no evidence of her, either. He passed Abigail in the hall leading to the backdoor, without so much as a word of acknowledgement to her presence. *The horses.* Seconds later, he was moving through the gate, across the pasture to the barn. All the horses were accounted for. *The loft.* A quick run up the ladder confirmed her absence. *The cottage?*

The empty cottage led him back to the west wing of the mansion, as another search of the rooms would be futile. He returned to the kitchen exhausted and winded. "Eloise, where is she?"

"Who, sir?"

"Livy. Where has she gone?"

"I am sorry, sir; I have not seen her."

Miles entered carrying a periodical.

"Miles, has Miss Nichols ordered a carriage?" Hiram asked in desperation.

"No, sir. I have not seen Miss Nichols."

Hiram caught his breath and ran toward the main entrance. He stepped out on to the portal. The landscape revealed nothing.

Dr. Lambert approached him from behind. "Mr. McDonnally, yer niece is fine. Not to worry."

Hiram turned, "How is she?"

"In need o' rest and better nutrition. Accordin' to her husband, Sophia has been eatin', but not the proper foods."

Still preoccupied with Livia, staring blankly, he asked, "Proper foods? Have you seen Miss Nichols?"

"Only briefly, outside o' Sophia's room when I arrived."

Hiram let out a frustrated sigh and dropped to the steps where he sat cradling his head in his hands. "She's gone...Why me? Why does it continue to happen to me? I think that I have been cursed," he mumbled.

The doctor stood over him. "From where I stand, the only things that you have been cursed with are a loving family, good looks, charm, social position, and wealth."

Hiram looked up.

"Son, she couldna hae gone far."

"Rahzvon was right...she deserves better."

"Ye o' little faith...Good day, Mr. McDonnally."

Hiram watched the physician's cart move toward the end of the drive and remained there for several minutes before returning to his study. Kade was gone—and now Livia. He was truly alone.

Twenty minutes later, he answered the rapping and flew to the doors, "Livy?"

"No, Hiram," Abigail replied, "I was waiting in the parlor. I thought I might visit my brother. Mrs. Zigmann said that he is visiting at Brachney—"

"That's it!" Hiram tore out of the study like a bat out of Hades. "Visit him later!"

"Very well, I shall be waiting, darling!" Abigail called out to him.

Within minutes, Hiram was summoning a coachman to drive him to Brachney Hall and instructing Eloise to make up a room for Abigail.

Exhausted from the walk through the woods and the anxiety of seeing Hiram with Abigail, Livia had taken refuge in Naomi and Edward's guest room. Downstairs, Hiram was invited in, where he did not hesitate to inquire of Livia's presence.

Naomi took a hold of his arm. "Now, Hiram, Livia is not up to seeing you at this time. You have to honor her wishes."

"I do not have to honor anything—have you not heard? I am not an honorable man!"

Edward stepped from the foyer. "Watch your tone, Hiram."

Hiram ran his fingers back through his hair. "Naomi, I apologize...I must see her."

"We cannot allow it, Hiram. Come talk with us in the study," Edward offered, placing an arm over Hiram's shoulders.

"What did she tell you?" Hiram asked.

"Nothing, except that she asked to stay the night and not to be disturbed by anyone—especially you," Naomi explained.

Hiram paced around the library table. "My life continues as one long chain of unjust, unexpected predicaments. One minute, I was playing in the loft—I mean, in the barn with Livy. The next, Miles is below, announcing her arrival. There I was comforting Abby when—"

"*Abby?*" they questioned in unison.

Hiram replied with dread, "Yes, my dear aunt and uncle, Abigail O'Leardon, sister of my dear friend Daniel, has returned to Lochmoor Glen to 'pick up where she left off', so to speak—leaving Lattimer by the wayside."

Naomi and Edward shared a look of mutual understanding to Livia's mysterious arrival.

"It did not end there. Nay, that was not enough! My niece's—our niece's husband has not only endangered Sophia's life and threatened mine, but had the gall to tell me that I am a worthless excuse of a man! Which I may be, but I did not need to hear it from him."

"Rahzvon?" Naomi said with disbelief.

"Oh, I am inclined to agree with him," Hiram nodded, "but I shan't ever forgive him for making that child into a mother!"

Naomi beamed. "I knew it. I thought Sophia was with child."

"Why are you smiling?" Hiram paused and demanded.

Edward cut in, "They are married, young, and in love. It is wonderful news for the clan."

"The clan? Is that your only concern? She has been put to her bed!" Hiram shouted.

"Oh, no. Is she having difficulty?" Naomi asked.

"She fainted. That husband is not seeing that she eats properly—great Scott she is eating every time I see her. Thank God she is no longer living in that biscuit tin...with tables hanging from the ceiling and sleeping on the floor like a stray dog." Hiram began pacing, again.

"Rest assured that Hannah and Eloise will look after her, now that she has returned," Naomi comforted.

Hiram threw up his arms, "And Abigail, do not forget her! She has made camp there, as well. And Sophia—she is thrilled about it!"

Daniel entered the library with Beatrice. "Abby is here in Lochmoor Glen?"

"Aye, I have to see Livy." Hiram left to find her.

"You are making another mistake!" Edward called to him.

"So me sister and her husband are visitin'," Daniel said with apparent surprise.

"I think not...I believe that she has come alone," Naomi said with concern.

***

After trying several doors, Hiram found Livia asleep, curled up in a chair in a bedchamber with the heavy curtains drawn. Stepping closer, he noticed that her head was uncomfortably positioned. He gently lifted the exhausted woman to the bed and covered her with the quilt.

Edward and Naomi sat in the parlor. Edward read while Naomi knitted booties for the future baby Sierzik, a gift initially for Kade. They strained their ears for a quarter hour. Naomi stopped rocking.

"Dear, perhaps you should go upstairs."

"And do what—interrupt a moment of reconciliation? My dear magic square, they, like us, are hopelessly in love."

"Livy! Come back here!!"

Naomi and Edward grimaced as the shouting drew nearer. Naomi cast on a quick dozen stitches.

"Make no demands on me, Hiram Geoffrey McDonnally!" Livia called back as she ran down the stairs. "Agh! Do not touch me! Unhand me—you brute!"

"I shall touch you, anytime I shall see fit!"

Edward cleared his throat and loosened his collar. *Perhaps, I should intervene,* he questioned.

Naomi dropped her knitting to the basket and nervously walked to the mantelpiece and picked up a candlesnuffer and examined it.

"Please move out of my way, Hiram. I am leaving!" Livia commanded.

"Never. You are staying right here until I am finished explaining. I shan't take orders from anyone!"

Perhaps now is not the time, Edward reconsidered and left his chair to join Naomi. He led her quietly to the library.

"Mr. McDonnally, I am not even slightly interested in your feeble, creative explanations. I have eyes and ears. I have seen and heard all that I care to for one day—probably enough to last me the rest of my life!" She pushed on his forearms, which remained solidly positioned.

"Abigail arrived uninvited and unannounced."

"How is Sophia?" she demanded.

"She will be fine."

"Has she gone?" Livia asked sharply.

"Sophia?"

"No; you know to whom I am referring."

Hiram's jaw tightened. "She shall be leaving tomorrow... probably."

"Tomorrow, *probably*?"

"Well, she desires to see Daniel."

Daniel entered the front hall at that moment. Hiram lowered his entrapping arms.

Daniel announced in a reserved tone, "Hiram, I shan't be seein' ya for dinner. I am goin' to visit Abby. Would she be stayin' at the inn?"

Hiram felt the flush creep up his face. "Uh, no... I believe she will be staying at the...the mansion tonight."

Livia made a sharp about-face, nearly colliding with Angus walking toward her. "Angus, please drive me to the inn."

"Livy! Livy it is an enormous house. There is room for dozens of women!" he shouted to her.

"Yes, and you seem to collect them like Edward collects stamps!"

"That comment was *not* necessary. Very well, go to the inn! Stay there until you realize that I am the only man that you have ever loved or ever shall!"

The back door slammed behind her.

Chapter XII

"Strikes Twice"

"Pleasant summer over
And all the summer flowers,
The red fire blazes
The grey smoke towers."

—Robert L. Stevenson

After arriving at his home in record time, Hiram marched inside.

"Nay, this is not happening," he grumbled.

Darting upstairs with the intent to end the madness, he approached the guest room where he could hear Abigail humming merrily. He paused. *I have control of my life. I will go in there and...what shall I say?* He stood for a minute more, listening to the very-much-at-home guest. He clenched his fists and left to his room.

After a quick wash and a clean shirt, he affirmed, *This is my life and I make the decisions.*

The man, feared by all, entered the inn, "What room has Miss Nichols let?"

"Number five, sir, but she asked that she not be...be disturbed?" the innkeeper said weakly.

"That is my concern now, not *yours*. How many guests are registered here?" He grabbed the registry book and examined it.

"Only Miss Nichols, but I am expect—"

"You are expecting no one. Go home. The inn is closed."

"Forever?" the innkeeper asked with dread.

"Possibly, if you ask any more questions and do not get out of here." He slammed the book to the counter.

"But, sir," the innkeeper pleaded.

There was no need for further discussion; the threatening expression sufficed. The proprietor snatched his cap, threw the keys on the table by the door, and exited with the speed of a hunted fox. The determined intruder locked the door, posted the closed sign and took the keys to Room 4.

A half hour later, Livia left her room, 5, to get something to eat. The dining room was empty.

Within a minute, she realized that the innkeeper was "off duty" and the establishment uncommonly quiet. A glance to the door with the "open" side of the sign in view, she paused. *I will ask the other patrons,* she thought turning to the counter. She leafed through the registry. She looked up with curious suspicion. Her name was the only one recorded. "Hmm? I guess he has gone out on an emergency of sorts," she mumbled. She started back to her room, when she noticed that the door for room Number 4 was cracked open. She froze in her position again. She cocked her head and listened. *There is someone in there.* She moved quickly to the wall, breathing as shallow as possible. With sleuth-like motion, she gingerly slid along the wall to the doorjamb. Her heart was racing a mile a minute. She peeked inside. Her jaw dropped. She pushed the door open.

"What are *you* doing here?"

Hiram resisted his natural instinct to rise when she entered the room. Dwarfing the little writing table, he continued scribbling on a paper. "Whatever I so desire."

To appear unaffected by his bluntness, she asked casually, "What are you writing?" She strolled to the bureau, where she saw a shirt rolled upon it.

"I am composing a list."

"A list of names of women to add to your collection?"

Hiram placed the pen in the well and sat back in the small chair that creaked under his weight. "This is my room, Miss Nichols. If you care to criticize, you may leave." He resumed his writing.

Now, unaffected by his sharpness, she asked nonchalantly, "How long do you think that you shall be writing?" *That was a silly thing to ask,* she regretted.

"Until I am finished."

She walked back to the bureau, trying to steal a glimpse of the list. His broad shoulders blocked any sneak preview. She picked up his rolled shirt on the bureau and instinctively put it to her nose, in anticipation of that glorious cologne. Realizing her weakness, she replaced it instantly and returned to the chair. *Why the extra shirt?* "A list, you say? A monumental list of my faults and failings?" she asked brazenly.

At that very moment, a thunder crash replied. Hiram dropped the pen to the well, again, and turned giving her a raised brow, suggesting that perhaps the Heavens above disapproved of her continued insolence. He handed her the list, walked over to the bed and stretched out. His unnerving expression led her to focus on the paper, which she read silently.

Invitations
Flowers (dozens of bouquets of the freshest found)
Music (stringed quartet/Joseph, pipes)
Dress (imported from Paris)

A cold shiver ran through her as she continued to read. She looked to the bed. His countenance was stern, intimidating, and unaltered.

Carriage
Gray horse
Tartan
Passage
Food (plenty)
Rings
Rice

She looked to him again. A wedding list. But for whom? Could he be so cruel? Was this his way of telling her, that he and Abigail were reunited and to wed? She continued reading. Her hands began to tremble.

Large clock
Toad

Stunned, she looked up to see his open hand. She stared at it, then at the window pounded by the driving rain. Another thunder crash made her jump. Hiram appeared unaffected.

With his hand still outstretched, he demanded, "Give it to me."

She handed him the list. He folded it, shoved it into his pocket and left the bed.

He paused in the hall, "Well, I shall say goodnight. I must go."

"Go—go where?" Livia's voice cracked.

"Home."

"But...the storm."

"A little water never hurt anyone. You should know—at one time, you had us standing in a squall in our best attire. Sleep well, Livy." Hiram nodded and left the room.

"Hiram!" she called out.

He stopped at the landing. "Aye?"

"Am I here, *alone*?"

"Aye, not a soul to disturb you. I even sent the innkeeper home."

"But he lives here."

Hiram paused and smoothed his beard. "Not tonight."

Livia trailed slowly behind him. The winds howled and the rain danced on the tin roof above them.

"No need to follow, Livy. Go back to your room. I shall lock up."

She ignored his suggestion and followed him to the dining room. Two loud thunder crashes that shook the little building gave her cause to steady herself at the stair rail.

"Hiram?"

"What is it, Livy?"

"I think that you should wait here until the storm passes."

"Nay, that could be all night. I really need to be going, I have a wealth of paperwork waiting. Goodnight, Livy."

And Abigail, she feared.

Livia left the staircase and entered Room 4 to extinguish the lantern when she noticed Hiram's rolled shirt on the bureau. She snatched it up and hurried toward the stairs. At the landing, she stopped, caressed the shirt next to her face, and returned to her room. She curled up on her bed with Hiram's shirt tucked under her head. "Please, God, see that he gets home safely."

With a crash from the dining room, she flew from the bed. Still clutching his shirt, she ran to the staircase.

"Hiram! Hiram are you injured?"

"I think not!"

Livia rushed down the steps where she saw Hiram righting a chair and rubbing his knee.

"What happened?"

"A wee bit clumsy, that is all. Goodnight."

Livia returned to the stairs. Hiram grinned. She tucked his rolled shirt next to her chest. He reached for the door handle, and then turned, giving her a look of anticipation. Livia remained on the step, stoic and immobile.

"Livy, I would suspect that you are uncomfortable with the storm and—"

"On the contrary, I adore a good storm; I find it to be inspiring and uplifting."

"Inspiring?"

"Yes, it makes me feel alive and part of the universe."

"Hmm? How do I make you feel?"

His dark eyes were luring her in. She looked away.

"Livy, come, sit with me."

She could not resist. She cautiously took a seat at a table.

In the east wing, Sophia sipped the warm milk that her husband had so graciously provided. He removed his robe and climbed into bed next to her.

Sophia held the warm mug with both hands. "My dear, we have servants. You did not have to trouble yourself to get this for me."

"Phia, if I have told you once, I have told you a thousand times—you and this child are my responsibility. For the time being, I am providing next to nothing for the two of you. The very least I can do is to walk down to the kitchen to fetch a glass of milk for you. Speaking of which, you heard what the doctor said—you need to eat more nutritious foods."

"Can I help that this baby prefers afters?"

"Phia, that is ridiculous. How would you know?"

"All children prefer afters. Her craving, makes me crave them."

Rahzvon dropped to the pillow in defeat. "We will discuss it tomorrow. I need some sleep."

"Why did Abigail return?"

"Rumor has it that she has left her husband and is back to reclaim your uncle. She can have him."

"That is blasphony."

"Blasphemy...just in case the children ask. Livia is too good for him."

"You are a poor sport because we are living here. You would say anything horrid about Uncle Hiram. Besides, Livia is madly in love with him."

"A pity it is not returned."

"Why do you say such absurdities?"

"If your uncle loved Livia, Abigail would not be staying here while Livia was sleeping at the inn."

Sophia put the empty cup on the side table and sat up. "*No.* Livia has moved out?"

Rahzvon put his arms behind his head. "Yes, I am sorry to say that it is true. Or maybe I am not. I do not understand the man. He had the love of the most beautiful, agreeable woman I have ever known and he let her slip away like a circus balloon without a string."

"Most beautiful—most agreeable?" Sophia's black eyes pierced his.

Rahzvon offered a quick smile. "For a woman of her age."

"Oh." Sophia slid down beneath the covers and snuggled her arm across his chest. "Please, tell me... do you think that I shall be the most beautiful and most agreeable when I am her age?"

Rahzvon laughed. "Most beautiful? There is not a doubt. Agreeable? Little One you have something that Miss Nichols does not have."

Sophia grinned. "What is that?"

"The McDonnally blood running through your veins."

"You make fun, but remember your children

shall, as well."

"Do not remind me, Mrs. Sierzik." He leaned over and kissed her and blew out the lantern's flame."

"Goodnight, Mr. Sierzik."

"Goodnight, my beautiful wife."

At the inn, Hiram pulled out a chair, turned it around, and straddled it. Leaning on the back, he asked again, "How do I make you feel, Livy?" His unrelenting stare brought her immediate discomfort. "Do you not have a reply for me?"

A bolt of lightning struck in the street just outside the door. Livia jumped at the flash, and then forced a smile. "You make me feel uncomfortable."

"Aye? Me? The man who rescued you from incarceration with Warden Turvy—the man who gave you his home—the man who is funding your day school—the only man that you have ever kissed—the man who is always right? This is the man with whom you are uncomfortable?" He smiled, "The man with the beard that you adore?"

His dancing eyes and deep dimples were irresistible. She reached across the table and ran her fingers through his beard.

He stroked the back of her hand, "Now, love, please, tell me. How do you feel about me?"

"Safe. Secure."

"Then come along." He took her hand to the reading area of the lobby. He moved the couch to face the blurry window and offered her a seat. After turning down the lanterns, he joined her. The flashes of light created an incredible display. "Now we shall be inspired by the marvels of the universe together."

Livia snuggled under his arm. Hiram smiled

noting that she was still clutching his rolled shirt.

She looked up and said, "Our wedding list—you do love me."

He patted his chest where the list lay within his vest pocket. "Always have, and always will. Do you desire a long engagement, Livy?"

"It seems as though we have been engaged for ten years, but...I have not been formally ask—"

A loud rapping drew their attention to the front door.

"Can they not read the sign?" Hiram protested.

"It could be an emergency."

The rapping continued with a muffled cry, "Mr. McDonnally, open the door! It is urgent!"

Chapter XIII

"Fallen Hero?"

"Toiling—rejoicing—sorrowing,
Onward through life he goes;
Each morning sees some task begin,
Each evening sees it close;
Something attempted, something done,
Has earned a night's repose."

—Henry W. Longfellow

Hiram fumbled with the key to open the inn door.

"Jake, what is it?"

"Yer east wing is a fire! Half the village is there helpin'. The rain has helped a wee bit. Come, get in the carriage, I'll drive ye."

"Sophia—is she safe?"

"I canna tell ye."

Hiram led Livia through the plummeting drops. Jake closed the carriage door and sent the horses into a fast trot.

Livia and Hiram clasped their hands between them. Neither spoke, as fearful thoughts and prayers hastened them toward the estate. The dread of what may await them curbed their desire for an expeditious ride. When they entered the driveway, the enormous billowing smoke cloud hovering over the mansion heightened their fears. A series of relentless lightning strikes amidst the drizzling rain confirmed the ghastly silhouette. The roof was gone above the third floor in the east wing; the remainder of the structure seemed to be intact.

As they pulled into the drive, they saw Albert running toward them. Hiram was out of the carriage, in a split second.

"Sophia! How is Sophia? Where is she? Is she all right?" Hiram grabbed hold of Albert by the lapels, "Answer me, man! Has she been harmed?"

"Well, sir. She is well. Everyone is well, except young Master Sierzik."

Hiram looked fearfully to Livia. "Nay," he mumbled.

Albert took a hold of Hiram's arm. "The smoke, sir. He took in a great deal, getting Sophia out."

"Is he?"

"Not to worry, sir. Eloise thinks he shall be fine.

Dr. Lambert has just delivered a baby in the next village. He will be arriving, soon."

Hiram wiped his forehead. "Good."

"But, sir, it was not only the smoke. Poor lad burnt both his hands. Badly, I am afraid."

Hiram closed his eyes with the news; Livia fought her tears.

While they were hurrying toward the house, Albert explained that the fire was confined and in control. "Mr. McDonnally, we are concerned for Miss Sophia; she is hysterical with worry over Rahzvon."

They entered the parlor where they found Hannah and nearly all the women of Lochmoor doing their best to console Sophia, who was screaming and crying uncontrollably. Beatrice was sitting next to her, cradling Rahzvon's head in her lap, as he was stretched out on the divan. In a motherly fashion, she stroked the hair of her dear young traveling companion from many months passed.

Hiram and Livia moved through the crowd to where Sophia sat weeping in the rocking chair next to Rahzvon. Hiram placed a hand on her back, but could offer no words when he saw the damaged hands.

"Let me," Livia said moving in beside Sophia. She pulled back Sophia's hair and began whispering into her ear. Sophia's cries diminished to a few sobs. Livia pulled Hiram's handkerchief from his vest pocket and handed it to Sophia. Hiram, still focused on Sophia, casually retrieved the list that fell from his pocket, and laid it on the table next to him.

The room became remarkably quiet. Hannah, curious to the content of Livia's whispers, but grateful, touched Livia's shoulder. "Thank you."

Abigail stepped back. Her gaze moved from Livia, the woman whom she had verbally attacked at the boutique in London, to the folded paper that Hiram had placed on the table.

Rahzvon was waking, grimacing with pain from his blistered hands, between spells of coughing when Dr. Lambert arrived to exam him.

"Back again. Sorry 'bout yer home Mr. McDonnally," the doctor said, while listening through the stethoscope.

"Thank you. Walls can be replaced. How is he?"

"He has been to the devil and back. I shall administer something for the pain." He turned to Sophia. "Lassie, great care must be given to his hands. They need to be kept clean. There is a great chance o' infection. With proper care, there shouldna be a problem."

Hiram spoke up, "We will hire a special nurse. Sophia needs rest, as well."

"A good idea, sir. Now, I think once ye get 'im bedded down, ye all need to get some rest," the doctor suggested.

Hiram addressed the sympathetic faces peering from the hall. "My dear friends, we all thank you for your help and concern. Go to the kitchen. There is plenty to eat."

Livia left Sophia to her mother's care and spoke with Eloise on the way to the kitchen. Livia's eyes never met those of Abigail O'Leardon.

While Rahzvon was carried on a makeshift gurney upstairs to Sophia's old room, Abigail stood alone as the parlor emptied. She stared at the folded paper on the table and slowly inched toward it. She looked up with alarm when Naomi stepped in from the hall. Abigail folded the list and casually replaced it on the table.

Naomi stepped closer and smiled serenely. "He was not for me. He is not for you."

"I know; he loves Miss Nichols. And after seeing Sophia with Rahzvon, I realize now, that my place is with my husband. He is a soldier, you know. Naomi, would you mind if I spend the night at your home? I would like to visit with my brother before I leave tomorrow."

"Of course. I will send Miles up to get your things, while I fetch Mother. It will be difficult to coax her to leave Rahzvon. She is very fond of him and thinks of him as another one of her sons."

"Thank you, Naomi."

Abigail was packing when her brother, Daniel poked his head in the room.

"I spoke wit' Naomi. She says you're spendin' the night at Brachney Hall."

"Come in, Daniel. Yes, I do not belong here."

"Where do ya belong, Abby?"

"With Roland."

"Ya need to go to 'im directly. It has happened, Abby. Hiram just got word that King Albert requested help. Britain has declared war on Germany for invadin' Belgium."

"Oh, no!" Abigail snapped her bag closed. "Daniel, I am sorry I never got to spend more time with you, but—"

"We'll get together later. I'll be speakin' to Hiram. He will arrange for ya to go back to London immediately."

"Thank you. I love you, Daniel."

"Be safe and keep me informed. Give me regards to Roland."

"I shall."

The next morning, Sophia, sitting at Rahzvon's bedside, sipped her tea.

Edward cheerily entered from the hall with Hiram. "Good morning, lad, Sophia. How is the hero this morning?"

"Edward, Hiram." Rahzvon said, and then coughed. "Better, thank you."

"Not really," Sophia cut in. "He said his throat feels like he swallowed a steel brush and his hands like—"

"*Phia.* I will survive."

She moved next to her uncles. "It was positively terrifying. One minute we were in the sitting room—I was working one of those word puzzles, that you gave me Uncle Edward. I was perplexed by a five-letter word for a musician, ending in the letter 'R' while my poor tired husband was snoring on the couch."

"Piper," Rahzvon mumbled.

"Piper?" Sophia asked.

"The five-letter word," Rahzvon explained.

"That's it!" Sophia exclaimed. I knew it began with a 'P' from the word down, 'Pinochle.' I certainly feel better knowing that. Thank you, my darling." She patted his head. "As I was saying, all of a sudden there was a plume of smoke coming from the other bedroom. There were no lit lanterns in there, so I cannot fathom what started the fire. I guess it was lightning. Well, I screamed and rushed to wake my dear husband. Seconds later, it was dark, and the ceiling was caving in around us, and flames were everywhere! We were coughing and gagging."

Hiram embraced her, "It had to be horrifying. Thank God Rahzvon was with you."

"Yes, because then we found that we were trapped by some fallen beams. My brave husband pulled his shirt off and covered my head. I could hear his groans as he tossed the beams aside like matchsticks. He then scooped me up and carried me to the hall stairs."

"Very courageous, Rahzvon," Edward commended.

Rahzvon looked down. "Not really. How did the east wing fare? Was our bedroom lost?"

Sophia patted Rahzvon's shoulder lovingly. "My wardrobe—he is concerned about my wardrobe. Is he not wonderful?"

"The master bedroom was spared, with exception to the smoke damage," Hiram explained.

Rahzvon threw Sophia a brief smile. She stroked his arm. "It would not have mattered if my wardrobe had been lost; I have you, Rahzie."

"What? I was hoping it *was* lost, so that I would not have to move it again," Rahzvon said, grinning.

"Do you see? In this near death situation, he is still in good humor. Is he not positively perfect?" Sophia laid her head on his chest.

Edward gave a nod of confirmation.

"Aye, he is," Hiram said seriously, considering Rahzvon's heroic deed and the reprimand that saved Hiram's relationship with Livia.

"Thank you, sir. And the sitting room?"

"Not well," Edward said with regret.

"The desk?" Rahzvon inquired.

"Gone."

Rahzvon stared blankly for a moment contemplating its loss and the hidden note, and then looked up at Hiram.

"I never thanked you for the use of it. It was very generous of you. I am sorry that it was destroyed."

"You shan't be in the need of a desk for some time. It will be replaced with the finest that can be found. You saved my niece's life."

Rahzvon attempted to smile, but the pain in his hands had escalated considerably.

Edward started for the door. "Come along, Hiram, we have work to do and he needs some rest. Beatrice, will be reporting for duty, soon, so that this little mother can get some breakfast."

"Thank you for checking in," Rahzvon mumbled.

The two men nodded and left for the hall.

Sophia gently brushed Rahzvon's hair. "It shan't be long, darling. The nurse is scheduled to give you some pain medicine in the next few minutes." Witnessing his grimaces, Sophia nearly broke down, when she remembered Livia's whispers.

You love your baby. She hears you. You do not want her to be afraid for her daddy. She needs to know that you are not afraid.

Sophia pasted on a smile and addressed her stomach, "Little One, your father is quite the hero. Someday, when you are older, I shall tell you how he lifted the scorching beams to get us to safety. Right now, I do not believe you would know what scorching beams are."

Rahzvon closed his eyes and grinned. "Go eat your breakfast, it is important. Hold the stair railing."

"Very well, but I am not looking forward to it— breakfast, that is. I never thought there would be a day that the very sight of food would make me ill."

"It will pass, Phia."

Beatrice and the nurse arrived at the manor, simultaneously. Sophia left them in charge and went downstairs while Rahzvon rested comfortably after another dose of medicine. Beatrice closed the door and stepped into the hall to speak with Eloise in regard to the patient's breakfast. Rahzvon stared up at the canopy. *The desk is gone, but the blasted note is safe—I hope.* Its disquieting contents returned to haunt him. He recalled the last name of the author to be indiscernible—lost in a blurred stain. *Avera S.* He turned to the doorway where the two women chatted. The medication induced him to close his eyes and drift away from further thoughts on the subject.

Several days later, while Sophia and Naomi were organizing activities for the war effort, Livia entered the parlor where Rahzvon sat.

"Good afternoon, Rahzvon."

"Hello, Livia."

"You look like a lost lamb," she said sitting down next to him.

"Lost in boredom. Everyone is out there working together, while I am here, losing my mind. One would think that a holiday from physical labor would be a godsend, but this is worse than any task that I can imagine."

"You follow the doctor's orders and you will heal quickly."

"Hiram is doing enough for five men. Keep a close eye, Livia, he seemed near exhaustion the other night when he returned."

"Yes, but, as you know, having power over a McDonnally is next to impossible."

"True," he nodded.

"Rahzvon, we may not be very well acquainted, but we share a mutual McDonnally bond. With this, I have something that I need to share with you."

And I with you, Rahzvon's thoughts returned to the disturbing note.

"It is in regard to Marvel Wheaton."

"Ah, yes."

"What? She has spoken to you?"

"Yes. I am ashamed to admit that she is the one that opened my eyes to Sophia's condition."

"No...it is not that," Livia said looking nervously at her folded hands.

"Oh?"

"One day before the fire, Hiram and I were in the barn loft and—"

"Uh...Livia, I am not sure that our bond is quite that tight. Maybe I am not the one in whom you need to confide." He shifted uncomfortably.

Livia's face took on a light shade of pink. "Oh no! That was not what—no, Rahzvon!" She cleared her throat. "Later, when I was alone in the loft, I inadvertently overheard a conversation between Marvel and her sister Wilmoth...about you."

"What were they saying?" Rahzvon laughed nervously.

"Marvel told Wilmoth that she saw you hiding a letter from Sophia—in your desk."

Rahzvon sat up straight and took a deep breath.

"Rahzvon, I would have ignored the matter and I am aware that this is not my concern; I assure you that I have no interest in the content of the letter. I only felt that you should be entitled to this information...for Sophia's sake. Little girls find it difficult to keep secrets. I hesitated in mentioning this, with the desk being lost in the fire, but I..."

"I appreciate the information, but I do not want you drawing the wrong conclusions. In fact, you are the only person in whom I could confide about this letter." Rahzvon looked nervously toward the archway, and then leaned toward Livia.

Livia, now wondered if she cared to be *his* confidant.

"You must vow to discretion," he whispered.

"But Hiram—"

"Especially in regard to Hiram and Sophia."

"*Rahzvon?*" she questioned fearfully.

"Sophia cannot discover this."

"Cannot discover what?" Sophia asked entering the archway.

The two conspirators looked up.

"*Sophia,*" Livia said leaving her seat. "You nearly ruined the surprise."

"What goes on here? What am I not to discover?" she asked grinning.

"Well..." Rahzvon began.

"It is a gift for the baby! Is it not?" Sophia beamed.

Rahzvon and Livia faked their smiles.

"Then we shall pretend that this never happened. I simply adore surprises!" Sophia said latching onto Rahzvon's arm.

Livia and Rahzvon did not have the opportunity to resume their conversation about the letter, that day. It would have to wait until another opportune time.

Later that evening, Hiram sat hunched over his desk, surrounded by papers. His head lay resting peacefully on his folded arms.

Livia stood next to him, running her fingers through his curls. "My dear man, you need this rest."

Eloise entered the study. "The master's passed out, again?"

"Yes, Eloise. He cannot keep up this pace for much longer. He has been herding sheep, mending fences, milking cows at dawn, fixing wagon wheels, pulling lambs out of the mud and God only knows what else. Then he returns home to this mound and worry of paperwork."

"Oh, my carrot cake! Excuse me!"

While Eloise rushed off to the kitchen, Miles invited a visitor into the hall. Hannah stood on the staircase, observing. The guest admired the magnificent corridor while waiting to be announced. He ventured over to the grandfather clock.

Miles met Hannah on the bottom step.

"Madame—" Miles began.

"Is that him?"

"Uh..."

"Never mind, Miles. I shall take it from here. Go along. You may attend to your packing." The butler continued up the stairs.

Hannah approached the visitor. "Alas, you are here. A bit late—what is your name?" she asked pointedly.

"Desilama R—"

"Mr. Llama, I realize that may be your customary attire, but this will never do," she said, while examining his long mid-eastern robes. "However, you are much too tall—what I mean to say, is that the available uniforms are much too small."

Desilama grinned.

Hannah raised her brows at the uncommonly handsome man. "This is not a humorous situation—we need your assistance immediately. One of our servants took ill, another has gone off to battle and Miles is taking leave to assist his family in Glasgow. You will just have to mind your step and take care not to trip wearing those—"

"Madame, I can assure you that for many years, my people have managed quite well, wearing—"

"No matter. Now, my poor over-worked brother

is in need of a bath. He can barely walk, having worked the farms since dawn. Please draw him a bath and assist him up the stairs. Thank the Lord that Eloise chose someone large; my brother Hiram is of great stature."

"Mr. McDonnally?" he asked with concern.

"Of course."

"M' lady, I think that you should know that—"

"Is it not *enough* that the east wing is gone and the stench of smoke remains, while my son-in-law was nearly killed trying to rescue my daughter in her fragile condition? Now, Mr. Camel, I have to maintain some order in this shambles of an estate. Come with me," she ordered.

Camel? He raised a brow and followed her to the study.

"Excuse us—he shall assist Hiram upstairs and prepare his bath," Hannah explained.

Livia was astonished at the sight of the well-groomed, exquisitely dressed *servant* looming over her.

Hannah moved in next to her. "I know; we shall have to have a uniform custom fit, but his size is an asset; he shall have little difficulty assisting Hiram."

Livia nodded in agreement, watching the extraordinary man coax Hiram to stand and aid him in the walk to the hall.

"Come along, Mr. McDonnally."

"Help him out of those filthy clothes and prepare his bath!" Hannah shouted as they continued up the steps.

Eloise met Livia and Hannah in the hall outside of the dining room.

"Shall I fetch Albert to help the master to bed?" Eloise asked.

"No, the new butler just took him upstairs,"

Hannah said looking at her pendant watch.

"New butler? When did he arrive?" Eloise asked. "He was not due to come until tomorrow."

"No, he is here. A good choice—quite a large man," Hannah said, closing the lid of her watch.

Eloise smiled at Livia. "Well, Miss Nichols, how does it feel having a guest from home?"

"From home?"

"Why yes, that is why I chose him. He is an American."

"I would have never guessed. From where is he, originally?" Livia asked.

"Iowa."

"I mean which country—where was he born?"

"America—Miss Nichols, you are aware that Iowa is in America?" Eloise looked confused.

"Yes, but from his appearance, one would have imagined him to be from some exotic region, such as India."

Hannah chimed in, "Yes, those robes are beautiful, but of little utility for his profession. He needs a uniform immediately."

"But Mum, I supplied him with three, last week when he accepted the position," Eloise explained.

"Well, he certainly was not wearing them, today."

"I will speak to Roy, immediately," Eloise said mounting the steps.

"Roy?" Hannah called to her.

"Yes, that is his name. Roy Weston. Did he not tell you?" Eloise asked leaving to locate the insubordinate servant.

Livia looked curiously at Hannah whose face now emulated a pale, lemon-eating child's. "Hannah, is something wrong?"

Hannah grabbed Livia's arm. "Livia, please ring

for Miles...I cannot," she mumbled, with difficulty breathing.

Livia did so and Miles appeared on the landing and ran down to the women.

"Miles... who is he?" Hannah asked fearfully.

"Who, Mum?"

"That man—in the robe?"

"Why, Mum, did he not introduce himself? He is Master Desilama Raheleka, a close friend and business associate of Master Edward."

Livia's jaw dropped and Hannah nearly passed out. Livia steadied her.

"Oh dear, what have I done? Hiram will show me no mercy," Hannah said lowering her head briefly, and then looked up with a start. "Quick, Miles, fetch that man! He is up with my brother...offer him some tea or...some cake...something!"

Hannah wiped the perspiration from her hands on her skirt and ran down the hall toward the backdoor. Livia and Miles stared curiously at one another.

The next morning, everyone sat at breakfast with the visitor—with the exception of Hannah.

"Sophia, what is detaining your mother?" Hiram asked and winked at Mr. Raheleka.

"She will be here, shortly, I am sure," Sophia replied looking queasy at the sight of the steaming bangers on the plate before her.

"Rahzvon, how was your breakfast?" Hiram asked.

"Excellent. I feel privileged being served first and fed by my loving wife." He smiled at Sophia who was looking a slight shade of green.

"Excuse me," Sophia ran from the room.

"She has discovered that our baby does not like breakfast anymore," Rahzvon explained.

Desilama nodded. "Well, I hope it soon passes and your injuries heal quickly. I understand that I missed seeing your brother Gaelon."

"Thank you for your good wishes, sir, and yes, Gaelon has left to sort out his affairs in Brussels. With the attack on Belgium, he has his work cut out for him. I had hoped that he would have remained here, until it was safe." He noticed Hannah in the hall moving very slowly. "Here's my mother-in-law, now."

The men rose at her entry.

Chapter XLV

"Sold?"

"Before criticizing a man,
walk a mile in his shoes."

"Hannah, I believe that you have met the honorable Mr. Desi*lama* Raheleka," Hiram said tersely, when she entered the dining room.

"I am honored, sir," she said humbly and stepped over to the table.

"May I?" Desilama offered to seat her.

Hannah closed her eyes with dread, "Thank you, sir."

Desilama grinned and picked up the toast caddy. "May I *serve* you Madame?"

Mortified, Hannah slid from her chair and fled from the dining room. Realizing his joking was in poor taste; Desilama quickly apologized and excused himself to make amends.

Hiram glanced around the table. "Ah, I guess it is only the three of us for breakfast." He looked to Rahzvon sitting idle, "My mistake—the two of us. Eat up, Livy."

Desilama found Hannah in the parlor. "Madame, please forgive me. I was foolish. I truly beg for your forgiveness."

Hannah sighed despairingly, "Sir, it is I who must apologize. I offer no excuse for my ignorant assumption—a distinguished man such as yourself, being subjected to such disrespect and—"

"Miss McDonnally, it was an innocent mistake. I will gratefully accept your apology if you will do me the honor of beginning this relationship, again."

"Sir?"

"Let us forget all that has transpired between us and return to breakfast with our gracious host as though we have just met." He offered her his arm.

She hesitated, took his arm, and smiled nervously up at her appealing escort. "I would like that."

At the close of the meal, after placing his napkin on the table, Desilama commented, "I have never enjoyed such fine cuisine, since I attended the Café de Bleu."

At the mention of her restaurant, Hannah said cautiously, but with some cynicism, "That is very amusing, sir."

"Amusing? I do not understand. Have you been there?"

Hannah shook her head. She looked suspiciously toward her brother and then to her daughter who had returned, sipping from a small glass of milk.

"Mother, I did not tell him," Sophia said, wrinkling her nose at the glass.

Hannah turned to Hiram.

"Nor, did I."

"Who told you, sir? Eloise?" Hannah asked Desilama.

"Told me what?"

"Mr. Raheleka, being the former proprietor of the Café de Bleu, your compliments, although appreciated, are quite transparent."

"This is not possible—I have dined there a half dozen times. I swear that I never saw you there."

"Recently?"

"A year ago. I am certain that I would have remembered such a lovely face."

Hannah smiled and looked away modestly.

"Honestly, I have never seen you before my visit here."

"What meals did you take?"

"Only the evening meals."

"I served only until two. I spent the evenings in the kitchen."

"Miss McDonnally, let me reassure you that my

comment was genuinely sincere and I knew of no connection between you and the restaurant."

Hannah paused, "Well then, I am grateful for your opinion," she said proudly, admiring his charming smile.

During the following weeks, Hannah and Desilama became very well acquainted, while conversing together during the evening hours. Hiram was quite pleased with the budding relationship, as he never felt comfortable with Hannah's interest in Rahzvon's insolent brother, Gaelon.

The escalation of the war led Naomi and Edward to make several trips to Edinburgh to aid in a variety of war efforts. Many of the men of Lochmoor Glen and the surrounding villages, including Jake Kilvert, went off to battle. Rahzvon's hands were healing nicely while he remained at the manor with Sophia. Hiram continued in his self-appointed duty to assist the agrarian families with their farms.

Meanwhile, Livia hosted the grand opening of her day school, *School of Little Dreams,* in the lower west wing. After a week, Livia's enrollment had increased to nine, as many mothers were now running their farms. Rahzvon and Sophia helped coordinate the activities.

One morning, Sophia was placing the little bowls of porridge around the table, when Rahzvon left for the kitchen facility to speak with Livia. She seemed to be distancing herself from any personal conversation with him.

"Livia, I sense that you are uncomfortable with my presence, especially when Sophia and I are alone with you. I need to speak to you privately, about the letter I found. I want you to understand."

Livia lifted the milk pitcher from the table and

nodded. "The letter? I had nearly forgotten. Yes, I shall make the arrangements."

They returned to the common room where Sophia was refereeing a squabble between two four-year olds over the privilege of sitting at the head of the table.

"Livia, I think that this daily occurrence could be stopped if you had a round table instead of a rectangular one," Rahzvon suggested.

Sophia smiled with great pride, "Is he not a genius?"

Livia concurred, "Yes, that is a wonderful idea, but speaking with Hiram in regard to the school is nearly impossible. Our lives are running like two creeks, which never come together."

"Has Hiram ever come to see your school?" Rahzvon asked.

Livia said solemnly, "No, he barely has time to take his evening meal at ten."

"He is putting in long hours...I know that he would be very proud of your accomplishments here."

Sophia called out "Now, children! We are not eating until you wash your hands! Please line up at the basin!"

"Slow down! We are ladies and gentleman!" Livia reminded, and returned to the kitchen to retrieve another pair of spoons to replace those that were thrown to the floor in the skirmish.

Rahzvon followed Sophia to the basin. "Phia, your uncle needs to be told that he should take some time to see her school."

"I mentioned something about it in passing the other day. I believe he never heard a word." She looked past Rahzvon. "Erin! Miss, you know better! Please dry those hands before you return to the table!"

"Livia has worked very hard pulling this all together. She deserves better. He should show some interest—offer her some praise."

"Jeanie, please let go of my husband's leg and take your seat, we are preparing for grace." Sophia looked up at Rahzvon, "Darling, when are you going to speak to Uncle Hiram about Livia?"

"Me? Never. One reprimand from me is enough for a life time."

"Reprimand?"

"Nothing, Phia." He looked beyond Sophia, "Dara, please put your napkin on your lap, not your head."

"Perhaps, I could leave him a little reminder in his study," Sophia said, taking Rahzvon's arm and walking to the table. "Something subtle. Perhaps only the name of the school."

"Good idea—please put down those spoons, boys! They are not to be used as weapons!"

Sophia stepped next to Livia. "Do not worry, I will leave Uncle Hiram a wee bit of a reminder of your accomplishment."

Livia smiled, doubtful that it would make any difference.

Mid-morning Sunday was the only time set aside for Livia and Hiram. They vowed to accompany one another to the Sunday service unless an emergency arose, such as the Sunday on which the rotting tree fell on the McDougal's fence permitting the escape of forty-three sheep, or the Sabbath day that Hiram spent helping the widow Eanin rescue her chickens from a feral dog.

On this particular Sunday, Hiram and Livia sat together awaiting the arrival of the pastor. Edward turned from the pew in front of them and whispered,

"Hiram, why did you change your mind about the Garnett contract? We had discussed the advantages at length. The timing was crucial," he charged.

"You cannot purchase that which is sold," Hiram said sharply.

"We made that decision Tuesday—it did not sell until last night!" Edward's voice escalated.

"I beg to differ with you, but you are wrong—it was sold by Tuesday afternoon!" Hiram shouted.

"*Hiram,*" Livia took his hand and half-smiled at the dozens of faces now observing their every move.

"Well, it was," Hiram grumbled.

The pastor clearing his throat ended the debate and recaptured the congregation's attention for the rest of the service. However, the second the pastor had finished his prayer for those serving in battle, and had bid all a blessed day, Edward turned to his nephew.

"Tuesday afternoon? Where did you get that information?"

"From you, of course!"

Edward stood up, "What are you talking about?" his voice echoed through the church.

"*Edward,* please lower your voice," Naomi pleaded.

Little Timothy Eanin left his mother and ran to Hiram's defense. "Dunna yell at Master McDonnally! He is a hero, he saved me grandmama's chickens!"

"Thank you, Tim, for your support, but go along. I shall handle this." Hiram scooted him away.

"I never said any such thing," Edward growled.

"Aye, you did!" Hiram said through clenched teeth.

Livia tightened her grip on Hiram's arm and smiled nervously at the many eyes upon them.

"Are they gonna fight, Mama," one small girl

was heard saying as her mother hustled her out the door.

"How dare you pin this on me, Hiram!" Edward glared, pulling on Naomi's grip.

"'Twas as plain as that arrogant nose on your face, Edward McDonnally! Labeled across the contract—s—o—l—d, sold!"

"I left no such label!"

"Then, who did?" Hiram demanded.

S—o—l—d? Livia thought. She closed her eyes. *Oh no, Sophia's reminder!* "Come along, Hiram, get in the carriage, this is not the proper place for this discussion," she gently coaxed

"Noon tea at my house!" Hiram shouted.

"I will be there!" Edward called back.

"Trying to blame me, how dare he?" Hiram muttered helping Livia into the carriage. "He is well aware that only he and I have privy to those contracts."

Livia took her seat, "I am certain that it is only a simple misunderstanding."

"Simple misunderstanding? Do you have any idea how much money was lost along with the extraordinary opportunity to maintain financial stability?"

With tears now forming in her eyes, Livia turned toward the window to hide her guilt for the responsibility of a second failed transaction.

"Sorry, love," he took her hand. "I am spoiling the few minutes that we have together." He reached over and turned her face toward him. "Livy, forgive me. Now, tell me about your week. How are you managing with your little school?"

"School?" Livia said fearfully.

"Aye, what do you call it? *Little Dream School?*"

Livia bit her bottom lip and looked up with

pleading eyes, "No, *School of Little Dreams.*"

"Ah yes."

"*School of Little Dreams...*which could easily be abbreviated as..." She paused and waited for the explosion.

Hiram thought for a moment. The realization sent him to a sudden standing position—an unfortunate response in a low profile carriage.

"Agh!" He dropped to his seat.

"Hiram, are you hurt?" Livia panicked.

Hiram sat rubbing his head, moaning. He finally turned to her when the carriage came to a stop in front of the mansion.

"Livy, sometimes I would like to put you in a gilded cage where you would be safe."

Livia, lowered her head, "And the world safe from me?"

She barely finished her question when the carriage door flew open, presenting Edward's tormented expression.

"Out o' there, Hiram!"

Now, considering, Hiram's head injury and the recent discovery, Edward's demand was the proverbial straw that broke the camel's back. Hiram shot from his seat and was in Edward's face within seconds.

"Go home, Edward!"

"Hiram, I never—"

"I know—go home! You tend to take everything entirely too seriously. Man, there is a war going on!"

Edward stood in shock, "I...I."

"Aye! Go home!"

Naomi latched onto Edward's arm and nearly dragged him to their carriage while she called, "Good day, Livia!"

"I shall return!" Edward called out as Naomi

stuffed him into the carriage.

Hiram started walking down the side road toward the Dugan cottage. Livia ran to catch up with him.

"Are we going for a Sunday stroll?" she asked timidly.

Hiram's reply appeared in the form of knitted brows and a piercing glare.

"I guess, I shall catch up on my paperwork for the schoo—" she stopped and ran back to the mansion.

This was one time that Hiram would not cave-in to Livia's charming innocence. He maintained his pace.

After a quick trip to the west wing, Livia returned to plant herself in Hiram's study. Before long, she was lost in a sea of various scraps of paper strewn across the desk. Hiram entered quietly behind her, unnoticed. While Livia hummed merrily, he scrutinized all corners of the haphazard pile with near heart failure.

Chapter XV

"Self-preservation"

"There, in his mansion,
skill'd to rule,
The village master
taught his little school."

—Oliver Goldsmith

Hiram found quick relief in that the disorganized disaster upon his desk consisted of Livia's notes and receipts adorned with chicken scratches and scribbling, rather than his documents. Livia, unaware of Hiram's presence, was studying one two-inch strip when she stopped humming.

"I sometimes wish they would not pay in advance," she muttered.

Has she got a lot to learn.

She looked to the window, "Were the dozen potatoes for Erin's fee or was it the third smallest bundle of peat?"

Hiram watched her stir through the pile and pull out an ivory scrap.

"Ah, it was the potatoes...but fifteen instead of a dozen."

Huh?

Livia rummaged through the pile again. "Now where is that receipt for the bookcase...Oh, here are the instructions for the kitty project! Oh dear, here is that note for Eloise from Naomi." She stood up with her hands on her hips surveying the pile, "I really need that receipt to give to Hiram."

She continued rifling through the pile while Hiram watched in awe. He noticed a stray slip of paper at his feet and retrieved it. He read it and asked, "Is this what you are looking for?"

Livia nearly jumped out of her skin and held her hand to her heart trying to regain her composure.

"*Hiram,* you startled me."

"Sorry...what is all of this?"

"This? I hope you do not mind my borrowing your study," she said grabbing the wicker basket and dragging the piles from the desktop into it.

Hiram watched in disbelief, but Livia smiled up at him as she gathered the remaining papers and tossed them on top.

He grimaced. "Livy, put the basket down and come sit with me, over here," he offered, motioning to the far end of the room.

"Oh, we are going to sit in my little reading nook?"

"Aye, Livy. Please take a seat. We need to have a discussion." He pulled out her chair.

Livia braced herself for his scorn for the misplaced "S-O-L-D" note, which had been clipped to the contract. She vowed to take full responsibility and never reveal Sophia's part in the matter. She would protect the little mother at all costs.

"Love," he began gently. "I have obviously neglected you of late. I take full responsibility for this unfortunate error. I failed to respond to your one plea—the 'sold' reminder on my desk."

Livia smiled sweetly, relieved by his generous attitude.

"About your bookkeeping, Livy, and I use the term loosely, you no longer have to concern yourself with it."

Livia's smile faded. "I shan't?"

"Nay, Love, I shall handle it for you."

"Oh no, Hiram. You have enough with the farm work and your own financial affairs. I am managing very well by myself. My father said you can teach yourself anything, given enough time."

Hiram chuckled and shook his head, "No one has that much time."

Livia cocked her head, unsure of the remark. "I really am in no need of your assistance. Besides, there are things that you would not understand—you would be confused."

"Confused? My dear, do you have any conception of the magnitude of my dealings?"

"Hiram, this time *I* am right. Now, for example, would you understand that one of my student's tuition is paid every three days in a dozen eggs? Give or take two—depending on the hens laying capabilities. She is funny about laying after a storm. And you would not know that on the fourth day, they pay the remainder in cash. Another student attends only on the odd days one week and on the even days another...unless it rains and he shan't come until noon because his father needs the cart. Do you realize that this changes with each calendar month, as the odd and even numbered days change? These little details affect my billing system, you know," she said pointedly.

Hiram listened in utter amazement before he closed his eyes and rubbed his forehead.

"Hiram? Are you ill?"

He opened his eyes and leaned back. "Livy, where are we sitting?"

"In the reading nook which I designed."

"Where is that located?"

Livia took on a worrisome expression, "Uh...right here in your study."

"Where Livy?"

"In McDonnally Manor?"

"Aye, Livy. In my home, *our* home, I am a stickler for organization and excellent records. I abhor chaos, in all aspects of my life—especially in business and under this roof."

"Do you need my assistance?"

Hiram wiped his hand across his beard. "Livy, your intentions and efforts are admirable, but in good conscience, I cannot stand by and allow you to trouble yourself with this method—this time consuming procedure. Do you understand?"

"Yes, but I—"

"Livy I am always right, remember?"

"Yes, Hiram."

"Now, tomorrow, I have an hour open. Meet me here at four for tea. Bring your basket."

"Yes, Hiram. Hiram?"

"Aye?"

"Do you want me to bring an itemized list of the crocheted articles, completed and incomplete?"

"Crocheted articles?" Hiram squinted.

"Yes, Mrs. Meyers pays in crochet—a little for each day, except for half days on Fridays. She is knitting a multi-colored shawl with letters of the alphabet for the...the," she paused seeing Hiram's disapproval mount, "for the students," she mumbled.

Hiram stared blankly at her.

"Very well, then, I shall." She forced a smile and slid from her chair. She stepped next to him and stroked his sleeve, then the top of his hand, admiring his unusually strong grip on the chair arm. He snapped back to reality and took hold of her hand to guide her in front of him. He placed his hands on her waist.

"Livy, every day that I waken, I wonder how it is, that I was blessed with such an unusual woman. Then, I realize that these innumerable tests that you put me through were designed solely to strengthen my character. Because of you, Livia Nichols, and my love for you, I can face each arduous day, knowing that there is no task too great for me. You have shown me that, time and time again. Now, I have proof that you will continue to present me with more challenges than any man dare imagine. Even being a pacifist, I could probably fight this war single-handed."

"Are you certain that you are pleased with this arrangement?"

"I am ecstatic." He leaned forward and kissed her to show his *questionable* eternal gratitude. "Not only will I act as your accountant, I shall also pay a visit to your school while it is in session," he said taking care to touch her face gently, as his hands were quite rough.

"Nothing could please me more," she said smiling ear-to-ear. *Except a proposal.*

As requested, Livia arrived the next day with her unconventional filing cabinet. At the doors to the study, Hiram greeted her with a loving embrace and kiss. "Come, Love, over here." He offered her a chair by his desk, which was neatly arranged, displaying a new ledger, pen and ink. His positive attitude and good spirits were apparent, despite the intolerable condition of Livia's records.

"Now, Livy, I want you to listen and answer each of my questions accurately and quickly. I have but one hour available."

"Yes, Hiram."

"Let us get started. First of all, I need a list of your students." He opened the ledger and took the pen in hand. "Livy?"

"Full-time or part-time."

Hiram smiled. "Both."

"What do you consider to be full-time?"

"Those children enrolled for a full day." Hiram waited with his pen poised.

"A full day, every day, five days a week?"

Hiram returned the pen to the well and sat back. "Livy, I have one hour, less now. Please." He picked up the pen.

"Jeanie Wheaton."

"Jeanie...Wheaton. Very good. I will alphabetize them later. Next?"

"That is it."

"That is it?"

"She is my only full time student. Some go home a half hour early, others a quarter hour. Some stay an hour after the school is closed. Well, it is not really closed, as long as they are there. I have to charge each parent differently."

Hiram lowered the pen to the well, again, and stroked his beard, dreading the next fifty-five minutes, despite the excellent company with whom he would be sharing it.

Fifty minutes later, with the welcoming chime of the grandfather clock in the hall, Hiram closed the ledger. "Enough for today." He clenched his teeth and offered one last contemptuous look toward the disturbing basket, which held ninety percent of the remaining "documents" in need of recording.

It had been unquestionably, the longest hour of Hiram's life. Livia's unique, convoluted system was nothing less than mind-boggling and excruciatingly frustrating. At the end of the meeting, the two left in clearly opposite states of mind. Hiram was exhausted from the countless details and the struggle to remain calm. He nearly lost all control when she explained her amended credit system for those particular students who paid in potatoes on days when mashed potatoes were served at the noon meal. Livia on the other hand, left the study carefree and content with the outcome.

Hiram closed the doors, trying to put the entire nightmare behind him, with hopes of enjoying his dinner. He found himself actually looking forward to the farm chores, which were not nearly as tasking.

Later that week, Livia was removing the dishes from the new round table. "Now children, it is story time. Rahzvon is going to read from Sophia's favorite book again, *Wind in the Willows.*"

"No, no we dunna want to hear it!" Jeanie exclaimed.

"Jeanie, you know that all of the students are looking forward to the next chapter." She turned to Rahzvon. "Which chapter is it?"

"Chapter three, *The Wild Wood.*"

"Not today," Jeanie whined. "We want to hear 'bout the wizard."

"The wizard?" Livia asked.

"Aye, Michael Scott, o' course," Jeannie explained.

Livia stood dumbfounded while the children began to chant the wizard's name, "Michael Scott, Michael Scott!"

When Livia looked to Rahzvon, he shrugged with no knowledge of the character. Likewise, Sophia shook her head.

"Children! Please!" Livia called out to the group who continued, ignoring her. It suddenly became very quiet when they focused on the large man standing in the doorway. Hiram cleared his throat.

Livia turned to see his dimpled smile and moved slowly toward him. "I understand he is a wizard of sorts," she said with embarrassment.

"Aye? Is this true, children—you would like a tale of the mighty wizard?"

All the children cheered.

"Do you object, Miss Nichols?"

"No, I ...I suppose it would be fine." she said apprehensively.

"Very well, then," Hiram walked across the room and pulled down the map of Scotland and motioned for the pupils to join him. Confused, Livia watched curiously as the children hurried to sit on the carpet at his feet. She and her assistants, Rahzvon and Sophia, moved quickly to sit down behind them.

"One moment, sir, Mr. Donnally," Erin, a very precocious five-year old, said with authority, and then left the group. She ran to the napping area and pulled a quilt from the first cot. She ran back and handed it to Sophia. "You hae better cover yer belly. This may be too frightenin' for yer baby." Erin looked toward Hiram. "Ye may continue, sir."

Sophia smiled up at Rahzvon, and then turned to her uncle who was now silent. Having witnessed the compassionate exchange, Hiram stared at Sophia. For the first time, he realized that it was so very real and truly wonderful—Sophia was going to be a mother. Her cheeks were full and rosy; her black eyes were twinkling. Rahzvon, father of this baby, sat close behind, allowing her to lean on him. They were a family. Hiram glanced at his patient audience, then at Livia. *A family.* A moment of sadness gave him cause to lose his smile. His gaze moved slowly toward Livia who seemed to know what he was thinking. Her compassionate gaze precluded the nod and hopeful smile that encouraged him to continue.

"So you want to hear about the great warlock and his *Book of Might.* Many know of Michael Scott, but far too few know of his assistant."

A little boy seated in front raised his hand.

"What is it lad?" Hiram asked

"What is a sistant?"

Hiram chuckled. "A helper. Mr. and Mrs. Sierzik are Miss Nichols' assistants."

The child raised his hand again.

"Aye, lad?"

"Are ye a sistant today?"

"Indeed, I am. Now, on with the tale. Mr. Scott had a very capable assistant. He completed his tasks very efficiently and quickly. His chores varied."

Hiram went on to explain the legend that the assistant was instructed to split and top off the Eildon Hills of Scotland, thus giving them the skyline they have today. Hiram pointed to their location on the map.

"The second task was another large one. The wizard told him to damn up the River Tweed with stones," Hiram said with enthusiasm.

The children were awed by the thought.

"He did it, and very quickly. This formed the great Kelso, the rocky ridge." Hiram found it on the map and directed the children to it.

"Now, the wizard was tired of being disturbed by his assistant. He was finishing these tasks much too rapidly, barely giving Mr. Scott a chance to think up another. So, the wizard thought and thought. Finally, he told his assistant to spin ropes out of sand. Can you imagine how difficult this would be?"

All of the children and the three adults engrossed in the tale shook their heads.

"Well, it was just that—impossible. How many of you have been to Berwick-on-Tweed?" Hiram asked.

Nearly all the children raised their hands, as did Sophia, who dropped hers quickly.

"Have you seen the shore?"

"Aye!" they squealed.

"Who wants to report to Miss Nichols what is there?" Erin jumped to her feet and said in a very confident tone, "The sand is all rolly with what looks like ribs." Sophia nodded in agreement.

"Excellent. That is where Michael Scott's assistant struggled to spin the sand into ropes. You see, the wizard never had to think of another chore for his assistant again, because he is still trying to finish the last."

Hiram pointed to the map locating the shore of the East coast. He turned to face the group. "And that is but one of the many tales of Michael Scott."

The children applauded and Livia stood up.

"Children, please thank Mr. McDonnally, and then line up at the door to go outdoors. You may take a toy with you."

For Hiram, Livia's smile was thanks enough, but the children gathered around him with a host of gratitude and then scampered off to choose balls, wagons, and the like.

"Hiram, darling, I cannot thank you enough for baling me out of that "sticky thicket" as you call it."

Hiram laughed, "You are quite welcome, but the term is 'sticky wicket'. But surely, you have some American folklore that you could have shared with the children. Perhaps that character, Chapman and the apples for hard cider," Hiram chuckled.

"I will have you know that Johnny Appleseed had some fine ideas."

They turned to a child across the room, who had burst into tears. Rahzvon was confiscating a jump rope—the source of the disagreement.

"Perhaps, you are right; maybe I should tell them how Mr. Appleseed believed that attachment to material things leads to unhappiness. That might end the ongoing battles over the toys." Livia said straightening the rug. "He also never tried to collect from his debtors."

"Quite the business fellow, eh?" Hiram

chuckled, raising the map. They walked toward the table.

"You go ahead and make fun, but I have a great respect for the man. He paid for unwanted horses and put them out to pasture, to save them from being slaughtered."

"I am sure the children would enjoy hearing about that," he teased.

They turned to another commotion by the door where Sophia was busy straightening the line of children, which resembled the sands of Berwick. A little whimper from the nursery then drew Hiram and Livia's attention.

"It is little Martha Wheaton waking up from her nap. I have her, just for the day. Maryanne was not feeling, well," Livia explained.

"I hope that it is nothing serious."

"I don't believe so." Livia started toward the nursery, when a boy of about four, grabbed her hand complaining, "I was to be the leader today, Miss Nichols—please tell Miss Sophia!"

"In a minute, Rufus." Livia looked anxiously toward the nursery where Martha was now screaming.

"It'll be too late!" Rufus begged.

"I can tell Sophia, Livia," Hiram offered.

"Nay, I want Miss Nichols to tell her!" Rufus frowned objectionably.

"Hiram, could you please bring Martha to me," she asked cautiously.

Hiram glanced nervously toward the nursery.

"C'mon, Miss Nichols," Rufus pleaded, tugging at Livia's hand.

Hiram's lips tightened and his brows knitted slightly. Livia could see his apprehension as he reluctantly nodded and walked toward the infant's frantic cries.

Livia followed the little boy's lead toward the line, but glanced back with concern to see Hiram pause before entering the nursery. It was his first encounter with a wailing baby since Kade left. Livia knew that the heart-breaking memory of their nearly adopted son was challenging his attempt to rescue Martha. *Can you do it?* she questioned.

With Martha's relentless cries, Hiram's fears surfaced. With each step, a new, disquieting thought arose. Did they know that Kade liked pacing? Did they sing to him? He detested bouncing. Did he wonder why he had abandoned him? *Are you waiting for me to return?*

Hiram stepped toward the crib where Martha was sobbing. She had pulled herself to stand, gripping the side of the crib rail. Hiram stood over her, staring at her. Trembling, he picked her up and started pacing with her, taking care not to bounce her.

"It is all right...Martha," he gently comforted her.

His words had no affect on her. She kept leaning from his arms reaching toward the crib. He turned to see the source of her interest. There it was peering at him from beneath. This was what she wanted. Hiram froze. She was nearly pulling from his arms when he held her close with one arm and leaned down to the familiar stuffed pony—his gift for Kade. He tucked it next to her. She held it close and stopped crying.

He stepped over to the rocking chair and sat down with her, cradling her in his arms. Her cries reduced to an occasional sob. She focused on his face and then reached up and touched his bearded chin.

"Do you like that?" he asked.

Martha smiled.

"A little lady with good taste."

She grabbed his shirtfront and struggled to pull herself to a sitting position. She laid her head against his chest. He watched her tiny hand slide down his sleeve to his hand. She latched onto his thumb.

He took a breath, relaxed and began to rock.

Hiram's calming song drew Livia toward the nursery.

She peeked in to see the serene infant snuggled in Hiram's arms. Martha was holding onto the pony like a life preserver in a storm.

I knew you could do it, Hiram. She looked to the heavens. *Thank you.*

From that moment, Martha Wheaton, proud owner of Kade's stuffed pony, held a special place in her heart for Master McDonnally and she in his. It would be many years before Martha Wheaton would learn that the "M" on her pony did not represent the first letter of her name.

"My fears, my tears, my cares, my sobs, and moans,
   In hope if ever I be to shipwreck driven,
   Ye will me draw to anchor in your heaven."

—William Fowler

Non-fictional facts referenced in Please, Tell Me

Sheaffer pen
Holy Grail-cup that Jesus drank from at The Last
    Supper/Sir Galahad recovers missing Holy Grail
Pendant and Gold/enameled French pocket watch
1610 Italian cabinets adorned with painted scenes
Monogrammed ecuelle, silver serving dish(1600's)
Ivory and walnut Lamentation statues(1750's)
German Dresden bureau
Baby Daisy vacuum cleaner (1910),
Hand-wringer washing machine—agitates both
    directions to prevent tangled clothing (1890)
Encyclopaedia Britannica Published in Edinburgh
Bean slicer (1900)
Strong box (17th century, Germany)
Quaich(double-handled silver cup/Scotland)
Automobile makes: Pierce Arrows, Columbia Baker
    Electric, Peerless, and the Argylls and Albions
    mfg/ Scotland
Jacob Riis- social reformer's quote p. 91
Wealthy Helena Zimmerman marries the bankrupt
    Duke of Manchester
Facts of venomous adders, grass snakes/Scotland
King Albert of Belgium requests British assistance
Ludwig Beethoven(musician)
American Girls Handy Book
Facts about Anna Held, wife of Mr. Ziegfeld
Painter Whistler's comment of actress Maxine Elliot
Actress Ethyl Barrymore- women imitating her voice
Review of actress Julia Marlowe
Actress Maude Adams reference to *Peter Pan*
Wind in the Willows information
Johnny "Appleseed" Chapman facts
Michael Scott Legends of Scotland's natural
    geography

220

Poetry Excerpts from the Chapters

Acknowledgements

British English A to Zed. New York: Facts on File, Inc., 2001.

Chronicle of the 20ᵗʰ Century. New York: Chronicle
   Publications, 1987.

Grun, Bernard. The Timetables of History: A Horizontal Linkage
   of People and Events. New York: Simon and Schuster,
   1982.

Illustrated Encyclopedia of Scotland. Anacortes: Oyster Press,
   2004.

Kidd, Dorothy. To See Ourselves. Edinburgh: HarperCollins,
   1992.

Kirkby, Mandy. Pick Your Brains About Scotland. London:
   Cargan Guides, 2005.

Lacayo, Richard & Russell, George. Eyewitness 150 Years of
   Journalism. New York: Time Inc. Magazine Company,
   1995.

Lochhead, Marion. Portrait of the Scott Country. London: The
   Trinity Press, 1968.

Petrie, Winifred. Folk Tales of the Borders. Edinburgh: Thomas
   Nelson and Sons Ltd., 1950

Summers, Gilbert. Exploring Rural Scotland. Lincolnwood:
   Passport Books, 1996.

This Fabulous Century Volume I and II. New York: Time-Life
   Books, 1969.

Webster's New Explorer Desk Encyclopedia. Springfield, MA:
   Federal Street Press, 2003.

Worthington-Williams, Michael. The Scottish Motor Industry.
   Great Britain: Shire Publications Ltd.,1989

Old News www.oldnewspublishing.com

I am a firm believer that education
should be an ongoing endeavor.
I stand by the unwritten law that education
should be entertaining for young and old, alike.
Thus, I incorporate
historic places, people, and events in my novels,
for your learning pleasure.

With loving thoughts,
Arianna Snow

To order copies
of the
Lochmoor Glen Series

Visit the
Golden Horse Ltd.
website:

www.ariannaghnovels.com

Watch for the
tenth in the series!